DESTINY

REVEALED

THE DESTINY TRILOGY (BOOK 1)

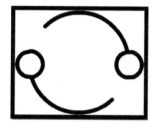

DESTINY

REVEALED

THE DESTINY TRILOGY (BOOK 1)

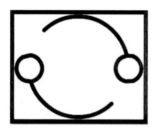

By: Cris Pasqueralle

TATE PUBLISHING
AND ENTERPRISES, LLC

Published by Tate Publishing & Enterprises, LLC
127 E. Trade Center Terrace | Mustang, Oklahoma 73064 USA
1.888.361.9473 | www.tatepublishing.com

Tate Publishing is committed to excellence in the publishing industry. The company reflects the philosophy established by the founders, based on Psalm 68:11,
"The Lord gave the word and great was the company of those who published it."

Book design copyright © 2014 by Tate Publishing, LLC. All rights reserved.

Published in the United States of America

ISBN: 978-1-63449-547-9
1. Fiction / Visionary & Metaphysical
2. Juvenile Fiction / Fantasy & Magic
14.08.26

Table of Contents

One

The piercing, joyful screams of pre-teens, just released from school on a Friday afternoon, filled the suburban neighborhood as they ran to a weekend of freedom, like zebras from a lion pride. One girl stood by the front door. She wore bright pink jeans, a tie-dyed sweatshirt, and held a backpack that matched her pants. The wind blew her long brown hair around her smiling face.

She saw a boy exiting the school. He wore blue jeans, a grey sweatshirt, and carried a black backpack. His face looked just like the girl's, but he had curly brown hair in place of her straight hair, was slightly taller, and carried the beginnings of an athletic build.

The girl sighed at her slow-moving brother.

"Let's go, Jack!" she said.

Jack shrugged. "What's the rush, Maddie?" he asked. "The house will be there when we get home."

"I want to start getting ready for the party," she said as she walked to him and grabbed his arm to hurry him along.

"The party's not till tomorrow," Jack said. "There's no hurry."

Maddie rolled her eyes. "You really don't know anything, do you?"

"No," Jack said. "I really don't care."

"You don't care about our birthday?" Maddie asked, as they started to walk home.

"Of course I care about *that*," Jack said. "There's a lot of great presents I want, but who cares about a dumb party?"

Maddie's eyes lit up. "The party will be great. Our friends singing happy birthday, cake, ice cream, and Uncle Benny will be there."

Jack smiled. "I like cake, and Uncle Benny's great, but I'd rather just have the presents."

Maddie pushed him. "You're a jerk," she said, and stopped walking.

Jack was about to give her a return push when he saw that she was looking at something behind them.

"What is it, Maddie?" he asked.

Maddie kept looking behind her. "I don't know. I thought I saw someone watching us."

Jack turned around. There were two parked cars, a tree, and an empty garbage can that had fallen over in the wind, but no one was there.

"I don't see anyone," he said. "Are you sure there was someone there?"

"I thought there was," Maddie said, and scratched her head. "And I thought I saw someone following us this morning."

Jack's eyes went wide. "On our way to school?!" he exclaimed. "Why didn't you say anything?"

"I don't know," Maddie replied. "I guess I was wrong." She looked around again. "There's no one there; let's just get home."

They walked for a few more blocks, Maddie talking about the preparations for the upcoming party, and Jack still looking around, wondering if Maddie did see someone watching them.

Hey," Jack said. "I know who you saw. One of the guys from One Direction must be following you to give you a big wet kiss for your birthday." He took a few steps in front of her and faced her so that he was walking backwards. Then he started making kissing noises at her.

"Oh, Maddie, we love you so much," he teased, every word punctuated with a kiss.

"Shut up!" Maddie yelled, and pushed him again. This time, Jack lost his balance and fell hard on his butt.

"Owww! That hurt," he said, and started to get up, but stopped when he saw that Maddie was staring across the street. "What is it?"

"Don't move," Maddie warned. "There's a guy in a blue hat, and he has his collar pulled up, so I can't see his face. He's standing on the corner; it's the same guy I saw this morning."

Jack was up on one knee, and he turned his body slowly so that he was facing in the direction of the corner. He lifted his head slightly so that he could see what Maddie had seen. He focused on the man standing on the corner; the man was definitely watching them.

"Okay," Jack said. "Let's find out what he wants." He shot into a full-run, in the direction of the man.

"No!" Maddie yelled, but Jack was gone.

"Hey, you!" Jack shouted as he ran, and the startled man took off.

Jack was in full pursuit and, when his prey turned a corner, Jack smiled. He knew this was a dead end street.

Jack ran hard, and when he turned the corner, he saw the back of the man as he ran into a backyard. Jack followed and saw the man duck behind a stack of wood in

4

the corner of the yard. He pushed off the ground, hard, to speed up, and took an unusually big step. Jack propelled through the air and landed on the woodpile. He looked down, expecting to see the man he had chased, but all Jack found was a blue baseball cap lying on the ground. Jack picked it up, and walked toward the street.

Maddie had just reached the front of the house as Jack came out of the backyard. She was breathing heavily.

"Where is he?" she asked.

Jack shrugged. "I don't know. I saw him hide, but when I got there, this was all that I found." He handed the cap to Maddie. "He just disappeared."

Maddie eyed the hat. "He couldn't have just disappeared."

Jack looked down. He wanted to tell Maddie about the chase and how he had gotten on top of the woodpile, but now wasn't the time. Something wasn't right. Jack didn't know what, but he knew something wasn't normal about what he had witnessed. People didn't just disappear, and Jack definitely couldn't fly.

He took a deep breath. "Come on, Maddie. Let's go home."

Maddie took a look around. There was no one in sight. She shrugged, dropped the cap, and headed home with her brother.

Two

Jack and Maddie walked the rest of the way home in near silence. Occasionally they talked about the upcoming party, but they avoided talking about what just happened completely. They finally reached home, a white colonial on a street with several other colonials of varying colors. There was a blue SUV in the driveway.

"Mom's home," Jack said.

"I wonder why she's home so early," Maddie thought out loud as they entered the house.

Inside the front door was a staircase with dark wood steps and a white banister. To the left of the stairs was a living room and, further down the hall, at the back of the house, was the kitchen.

Tina Austin, a woman with auburn, shoulder-length hair, creamy skin, light brown eyes that, in the right light, seemed to match her hair, and a smile that seemed to light the world, sat at the kitchen table. She was spooning dough onto a cookie sheet, and on the counter was a plate of warm chocolate chip cookies, which caught Jack's eye.

7

"All right! Cookies!" he exclaimed, and headed straight for them.

"Only take two," his mother said as he blew past her. "The rest are for tomorrow, and 'Hi, Mom,' would be nice."

"Sorry," Jack said through a mouthful of cookies, and kissed Tina on the cheek.

Maddie acted more civilized. She picked up a cookie, kissed Tina, and then joined her at the table.

"Why are you home so early?" Maddie asked.

"I took a half day so I could get ready for my children's thirteenth birthday party," Tina said. "It's a big deal, you know."

Maddie smiled at Jack. "I told you."

Jack settled into a chair at the table. "Here we go." He rolled his eyes.

"What's with you?" Tina asked.

Maddie answered for him. "Jack's too cool for a party."

"Shut up, Maddie!"

"We don't say shut up," Tina scolded. "And too cool or not, you're still getting a party."

She got up and put a tray of cookies into the oven. "So, how was your day?"

Jack and Maddie looked at each other, and Jack mouthed the word *no*. Maddie looked at him with wide eyes, and Jack knew that she would admit what had happened no matter what he wanted her to do.

"Something weird happened on the way home," Maddie confessed.

Tina closed the oven door and turned to look at the twins. "Like what?"

"Someone was following us," Maddie replied.

Tina sat between the twins, her face filled with concern. "One of the kids at school followed you home?"

Jack and Maddie looked at each other, and Jack shrugged. "I never thought of that," he said. "It was probably that freaky-looking kid who likes Maddie."

Maddie hesitated. "Maybe."

Tina put an arm around her daughter. "You don't think so, do you?"

"I don't know. It could have been." Maddie didn't sound so sure. "Jack went after him. Maybe he got a better look than I did."

Tina looked at Jack. "You went after him?!" she asked.

"Yeah," Jack replied. "If someone's following me, I'm going to find out why."

"Do you realize how dangerous that could have been?" Tina questioned. "There are a lot of crazy people out there, and they could be looking to hurt you."

"So, you don't think it was a kid from school either." Maddie directed her statement to their mother.

"I didn't say that," Tina corrected. "It probably was, but you have to be careful. You never know." She gave each of them a hug. "I'm just glad you're both safe."

"Don't worry, Mom," Jack assured her. "I'll always keep my little sister safe."

"We're the same age," Maddie argued, sounding annoyed.

Jack laughed. "Nope, I got you by seven minutes." He grabbed another cookie and headed to a small den off the kitchen where his prized video games were waiting for him.

"I'm going to do my homework." Maddie also took another cookie and left the room.

"I want help with dinner in one hour!" Tina called, knowing that her plea would go unanswered.

Three

Though it took nearly an hour, Tina coaxed Jack to help with dinner. He was chopping the last of the salad ingredients when a tall, thin man walked into the kitchen. Ray Austin had dark curly hair that was beginning to recede, and wore glasses. Jack dropped the knife and went over to him.

"Dad," he said, and gave him a hug.

"Now, that's a nice welcome," Ray said. Then he kissed Tina. "Where's Maddie?"

"Homework," Tina answered, and Ray nodded.

"Always the studious one; she doesn't even take a break for her birthday," he remarked.

"I think that's why she's being studious," Tina said. "She wants to take tomorrow off, which, by the way, is when their birthday is."

Ray smiled. "I think I know when my children's birthday is."

"Hmm," Tina moaned. "I wonder."

"How long till dinner?" Ray asked, changing the subject.

"Not long."

"I'll call Maddie, and we'll get the table set," Ray said as he went to the bottom of the stairs.

Maddie helped her father set the table, and the family shared a nice dinner. After their meal, Tina allowed the twins to start decorating for the party while she and Ray cleaned up. As he did the dishes, Ray noticed something strange about Tina. She seemed to be checking on the twins a lot as they cleared the table, and now she kept listening to what they were doing.

"Worried they're growing up too fast?" he asked.

Tina didn't answer right away. She stood at the entrance to the kitchen listening to Jack and Maddie bicker over how many balloons to hang in the living room. Ray put down his dishtowel and walked over to her, putting a hand on her shoulder.

"What's going on, Tina?" he said. "It's not like you to hover."

She took a deep breath, walked to the kitchen table, and sat down. "The twins had an incident on their way home from school today."

"What kind of incident?" Ray asked.

"Someone followed them and Jack tried to confront the person but he never caught up to him."

Ray looked over his shoulder to make sure the twins were out of earshot, and he brought his voice down to a whisper. "Who was it? Do we need to let Benny know about this?"

Tina shook her head. "I don't think so, but it got me thinking exactly what you're thinking."

"That we've been found," Ray said.

"At first, yes. I thought that might be the case, but there's a boy who likes Maddie, so it's more likely that he was following her and not the both of them." She paused. "It made me wonder about tomorrow. Do you think they're ready for all that information?"

Ray got up and took a bottle of water out of the refrigerator, taking a long drink. "They'll be thirteen tomorrow, and they need to know, or it's going to be a shock when things start to happen and they don't know why or how to control it."

"I know," Tina agreed. "But it's not like when *we* turned thirteen. They've been sheltered and they have a lot more to deal with than we ever did."

Ray sat down, put his hand on top of Tina's, and squeezed gently. "They'll be okay," he said. "They're special, you know."

She smiled. "I know."

After the house was decorated, everyone went to his or her room to settle in for the night. Ray stopped at Jack's room. He knocked but didn't wait for an answer to open the door.

It was a typical boy's room. There were sports posters on the walls, a mess on the floor, an unmade bed, and a video game on the computer. Jack's eyes were glued to the game, and his back was to the door as Ray walked in.

"You know," Ray said. "You're going to have to stop being such a slob; girls don't really like that."

Jack turned away from his game and faced Ray. "Who cares what they like?" he retorted. "I like it just fine."

Ray sat on the edge of the bed and smiled. "Oh, you'll care soon enough. Turn that off for a second; I want to talk to you."

Jack hit the pause button, and then faced his father. "What's up, Dad?"

"I heard you had a little run-in after school."

Jack laughed. "That weird kid who likes Maddie was following us, so I got rid of him; no biggie."

"You sure that's all it was?" Ray asked. "I don't need to talk to anyone at the school?"

16

"No, Dad; it's nothing. I can handle that kid if I have to."

"Well, let's not *have to*, okay?"

Jack grinned. "Sure, Dad."

Ray stood and rubbed Jack's head. "I like that you're looking out for your sister though, and I'm sure she's looking out for you, too." He walked to the door and turned back. "Don't stay up too late playing that thing. Big day tomorrow. Good night." He began to leave the room.

"Hey, Dad," Jack said, and Ray came back into the room.

"What is it?"

"When I was chasing that kid, something strange happened."

Ray walked back into the room and sat on the bed. "What do you mean by *strange*?"

Jack looked down at the floor and scratched his head; then he looked back at his father. "I chased him into a yard, and I saw him duck behind a woodpile, and I ran toward the pile and…" Jack hesitated.

Ray leaned forward. "Go on, Son; it's okay," he encouraged.

"It's stupid but... when I ran towards the woodpile, I felt like I was flying for a second, and I landed on top of the pile, and I didn't mean to..." he stopped, and looked down.

Ray lifted up Jack's chin so that they were looking eye to eye. "You know," Ray began. "When we're trying to protect someone we love, our bodies help us out and produce something called adrenaline, and that sometimes makes us able to do things we never thought we could."

"So it made me fly?" Jack questioned.

Ray laughed. "Relax; you're not Superman, but it's possible that a little adrenaline made you jump a further than you normally would. Our bodies are made like that to help us through dangerous situations."

Jack smiled. "Good; I thought I was weird or something."

Ray stood. "Oh, you're weird all right, just not a superhero."

Jack turned back to his game. "Thanks a lot, Dad."

"Don't stay up too late," Ray said while closing Jack's door as he stepped into the hall. He paused at the door for a second.

"They're ready, all right," he said to himself, and then headed to his own room.

18

Four

Ray walked out the last of the party guests and returned to the living room. He sat beside Tina on one of the loveseats and let out a long sigh. "Thank goodness that's over," he said.

"Excuse me?" Tina replied.

Ray cleared his throat. "Umm, I mean: great party."

Tina rolled her eyes and slapped Ray on the knee.

Jack and Maddie were seated on the couch beside a short, heavy-set, bald man. He was much older than Ray and Tina, but no one would ever call him elderly. He reminded the twins of Santa Claus, but without the beard. He brought them presents when he visited, told them stories, and made them laugh. They both loved Uncle Benny.

Benny took a small box from the inside pocket of his suit jacket; it was neatly wrapped in gold paper and had a small, silver bow on top of it. He then placed the box on the coffee table.

"Do you think you two can handle one more gift?" he asked, in his deep, gravelly voice.

The twins smiled the same dazzling smile of their mother.

"What do you think, Sis?" Jack asked. "Maybe we have too many presents."

Maddie shrugged and tossed her long hair behind her. "Well, maybe just one more," she answered, and everyone laughed.

"Very good," Benny said. "Why not one more? It's not every day we celebrate a thirteenth birthday—and two at once; that's very special." He pointed to the box. "Open it," their uncle urged.

Maddie picked up the box and noticed a small card attached to it. She read it out loud. "Happy birthday. Always believe in who you are. Stanton."

"Who's Stanton?" Jack asked.

Benny answered without hesitation. "A great man."

Ray cleared his throat loudly. "Yes," he said. "Stanton is a great man, and an old family friend."

"How come we've never met him?" Maddie asked.

"And why is he giving us a present?" Jack added.

Tina looked at Ray and then at the twins. She took a deep breath. "When you were born, Stanton had this gift made for you, but it was left behind when we came to this country."

Jack and Maddie looked at each other as if they were staring at a difficult question on a math test.

"We're immigrants?" Maddie said.

"You could say that," Tina offered.

"Open your gift," Ray encouraged. "Then we'll explain a few things."

The twins shrugged in unison, and Maddie tore the paper off the box and lifted the lid. Inside were two necklaces. One was a gold sun on a thick gold chain, and the other was a golden miniature of the Earth on a thin, gold chain.

"Put them on," Benny told them.

Jack put the sun necklace around his neck, and Maddie did the same with the Earth necklace. Jack looked at the box and saw that there was a second card inside. He picked it up.

"There's another card," he announced, and read it out loud. "The Earth will revolve around the Sun, until that time when the Sun is done. Then, the revolutions will be none, as their great power becomes one."

Jack had that math problem look on his face again. "What does it mean?" he asked.

Benny stood. "It means that those necklaces are very special, and you should never take them off. It also means that you two are very special and have a great destiny…"

Before Benny could say anything else, the house was engulfed in darkness.

The front door flew open and the party decorations were blown around by a small tornado that moved down the hall and into the living room.

Benny acted quickly. "Tina!" he yelled. "Get the twins out of here. Ray, prepare to fight."

Tina grabbed Maddie's hand and then Jack's, and quickly led them from the room and up the stairs. Benny raised his hands above his head and clapped them together. Instantly, the house was brightly lit. The tornado stopped in the center of the living room and, when the wind stopped, two men in red, hooded cloaks stood where the tornado was seconds before. Benny waved a hand and one of the men was thrown across the room. He crashed violently into the wall beside the fireplace and fell to the floor, unconscious.

Ray's attention was focused on the second intruder. He held out his hands, and the man was frozen in place. Suddenly, Ray's arms were pinned to his sides. A third man, cloaked in red, walked slowly into the room. He waved his hand casually, and the unconscious man got up, and the frozen man was able to move. Benny raised his hand but, before he could do anything, was knocked to the floor by an unseen force. The new intruder walked over to Benny and removed his hood.

His long white hair fell around his face, framing his hard features. He had old, gray eyes, sunken cheeks, and a chiseled chin. A chill that lowered the temperature of the room several degrees came from him. He looked down at Benny.

Benny's eyes went wide and he nearly choked on his own breath. "Tardon," he rasped. "I knew you'd come eventually."

Tardon smiled at Benny. "If you knew I'd come, Benjamin, you should have been better prepared."

Tina came running into the room. She stopped suddenly, and nearly all of her breath left her body at the sight of Tardon standing over Benny. She extended her hand, and a ball of white light was sent flying at Tardon. With just a glance, he deflected the light, and sent it exploding into the wall behind the couch, leaving a burning hole where it hit.

Benny took advantage of the distraction, and a flick of his wrist sent Tardon crashing to the floor. His companions were about to come to his aid, but Tardon was quickly back on his feet.

"Enough of this!" he yelled.

Tardon waved his hand, and a large bubble appeared in the room. Before anyone could move, Tina and Ray were encased in it. Maddie and Jack ran into the living room, and froze in their tracks when they saw what was happening.

Tardon saw the twins, but so did Benny. Before Tardon could act, Benny raised both of his hands, and a golden ring of light surrounded the twins. Tardon waved at the ring, and instantly pulled his hand back in pain. He waved again, in anger, and Benny was thrown across the room.

"Fool!" Tardon yelled. "You cannot protect them forever. Turn them over to me now, or I will kill their parents."

Benny closed his eyes and vanished, reappearing inside the protective ring with the twins. Then he put his arms around Jack and Maddie, closed his eyes, and the three of them disappeared.

Tardon growled his frustration. He clapped his hands and vanished with his assistants, as well as Ray and Tina.

Five

Cool air and the heavy smell of pine rushed at the twins as they appeared out of nothing onto a field at the edge of a forest. Benny began walking around as though he was looking for something, and tears ran down Maddie's cheeks. Jack tried to comfort her by putting an arm around her, but he couldn't control his own shaking.

Benny returned to them, and said, "Okay. It doesn't appear that we were followed. Come with me."

He began to walk into the forest, but the twins hesitated. Benny realized they weren't coming and stopped. Taking a deep breath and letting it out slowly, he said, "I know you've seen a lot that needs explaining—and I will explain everything—but right now, you need to come with me for your own safety."

Maddie looked at Jack, tears still running down her face. He gently squeezed her hand.

"Let's go," Jack said, feigning confidence.

They followed Benny into the forest, and the trees became denser and larger the longer they walked. Finally, Benny stopped in front of a large pine tree that had a trunk that was as thick as two elephants. He placed his hand against it and an opening appeared. Benny looked around again, and then motioned for the twins to follow him.

They walked inside the tree, and as soon as they entered, the opening sealed. The twins froze at the sight before them. It looked like a large apartment, not the inside of a tree, though it did smell strongly of pine.

The entrance led into a living room, sparsely decorated with only a black leather recliner, a small glass table that was piled high with books next to it, and a floor lamp. There were built-in shelves in all the walls and they were teeming with, what looked like, every book ever written.

Just beyond the living room was a small dining area with a small wooden table and four chairs that matched. A half wall separated the dining area from the kitchen that had all the standard kitchen fare. It contained a stove, a refrigerator, a sink, and a prep counter that looked as though it got very little use. There was a hallway beyond the kitchen that the twins guessed led to a bathroom and bedroom.

"Have a seat at the table," Benny said. "I'll get us something, and we'll have a talk."

Maddie had stopped crying, though her tear tracks were still damp, and Jack's heart pounded as if he'd just ran ten miles. He touched his sister's shoulder and guided her to the table. They sat down beside each other, and Maddie grabbed Jack's hand.

He forced a smile. "It'll be okay," Jack soothed. "Benny will tell us what's going on, and he'll fix everything."

Maddie took several deep breaths. "What was that, Jack? Who were those people? What happened to Mom and Dad? And what's happening to us?"

"Slow down there, missy," Benny said as he entered the room. He carried a small tray of mugs. He placed two mugs on the table in front of the twins, took one for himself, and then sat down across from them. "Let's have some hot cocoa and calm things down a bit."

Jack jumped to his feet and kicked his chair aside. "Calm?!" he screamed. "We just saw our parents locked in a giant bubble, strange people made things fly around our house, and you made us appear...." He clenched his teeth, and looked around at his surroundings. "I don't even know where we are, or how we got here."

Now it was Maddie's turn to comfort her brother. She stood, picked up the chair, and rubbed Jack's back.

27

"Breathe, Jack, breathe," she said, easing him back into his seat.

His chest heaved rapidly and he had a look on his face that Maddie had last seen when she hid his video games. She pushed one of the mugs toward him. "Drink some cocoa," she encouraged.

Jack took several sips of the hot liquid and it seemed to settle him down. Maddie also drank, and she, too, began to feel more at ease—relaxed, even.

Maddie looked at Benny. "Jack's right," she said. "A lot of strange things just happened and we'd like to know what's going on."

Benny nodded. "Of course; that's understandable," he replied. "But first, are you both okay? Physically, I mean. Are you hurt?"

Maddie looked at Jack, and then shook her head. "No, just a little scared."

"And a lot confused," Jack added.

"We'd just like some answers," Maddie said.

Benny took a sip from his own mug and leaned back in his chair. "Well," he began. "You are entitled to those." He stood and walked around the room for several seconds before settling back into his chair.

"You are thirteen and we were going to tell you anyway, but..." Benny paused for another sip from his mug. "The recent events have turned everything on their side." He let out a sigh. "Myself, your parents, and the two of you are not from the world you've grown up in."

Jack jumped up again. "Are you trying to tell us that we're space aliens?!"

Benny laughed. "Maybe I should have worded that better. No, we're not space aliens, but we are from a different world. Sort of."

Maddie had coaxed Jack back to his seat, and was trying to stay calm. "What are you trying to say?" she asked.

Benny sighed again. "The world that we all live in is divided into different realms of existence. The realm you know is the non-magical realm; there is a dream realm where nothing is real; there is a realm of thought, where ideas take birth; and there is a magical realm, where every magical creature you've ever heard of in stories truly exists. We are from the magical realm."

Maddie pushed her chair back from the table and looked at Benny, while Jack looked at the floor, scratching his head.

"Then, what are we?" Maddie said.

Benny leaned towards them. "You come from a long line of powerful wizards."

Jack stood and backed away from the table. "Come on, Sis," he said. "We need to get out of here, because this old man's nuts."

Benny chuckled. "That may be," he said. "But before you make any judgments, why don't you try making your cup come to you?"

Jack looked at Maddie and she shrugged. Then he turned back to Benny. "Don't I need a wand or something?" Jack asked.

"You watch too many movies, and read too many stories," Benny replied. "A wand is not necessary for your magic to flow. Just reach out your hand, think what you want to happen, and believe it."

Jack looked at the cup on the table, only a few feet away. He held out his hand and stared hard. The cup shook then, it took flight from the table, hit Jack's hand, and fell to the floor, shattering to pieces. Jack's eyes went wide as he looked at his sister, his mouth opened as wide as his gaze.

"Maddie," he said. "I...I did it."

"Yes, you did," Benny said. "I would have preferred that you actually caught the cup, but you did do it." He waved his hand and the pieces of the cup pulled themselves back together, and it returned to the table as though nothing had happened.

"Care to try?" Benny said to Maddie.

Maddie looked around and spotted a bowl of fruit on the kitchen counter. "Well," she said. "I *would* like an apple."

Benny smiled. "Then have one."

Maddie reached out her hand, and looked hard at the bowl. It spun around so that the apple faced Maddie, and then, one apple lifted into the air and floated gently across the room, landing softly in her hand. She smiled, almost giggled, at her newfound power. She took a bite out of the apple, and Jack patted her on the shoulder.

Benny clapped his hands. "Very good," he said. "I couldn't have done better myself." He stood. "That's enough for today; you two must be getting tired." As the words left Benny's lips, the twins began to yawn. "There's a bedroom down the hall, on the left. You can sleep there tonight."

Jack and Maddie didn't argue, or demand to know more about the events of the day; they simply headed down the hall without another word.

Benny went into the kitchen. A small house was nearly hidden in the corner of the counter. He knocked gently on the roof. Within seconds, a small ball of light emerged from the front door. It glowed brightly for a moment, and then, as it dimmed, transformed into a small man. He was no more than a few inches tall, and had butterfly wings.

"Jingo," Benny said. "I need you to let Stanton know the twins are safe, and that Tardon has Ray and Tina. I don't believe they are in immediate danger. I also need Connie here, as soon as possible."

The little man nodded and glowed brightly again. Benny covered his eyes from the blinding light and then, as if shot from a gun, the ball of light took off across the room and went through the wall without leaving a mark.

Six

The twins had no trouble finding the spare bedroom, and when Benny checked on them, they had already fallen asleep on top of the beds, too tired to even get under the blankets. Benny waved a hand and two blankets floated quietly out of the closet, unfolded, and gently draped over each twin. He closed the door, and went back to the dining room.

Seated in his chair was a young woman, barely older than Jack and Maddie. Her hair was dark brown, long, with red highlights only visible when the light hit them in just the right way. The girl stood when Benny entered the room, and her black leggings, black boots, and a gray hooded sweatshirt showed off her tall, athletic frame.

Benny was not surprised that she was there. "Connie," he said. "I guess you got here as fast as you could."

"I tried to get here faster," Connie replied. "But that fat Gnome still gives me a hard time whenever I come into the forest."

"Togo is just protecting the forest; that's what he does."

"Yeah, well he should know me by now," Connie said, looking past Benny and down the hall.

"Are they asleep? Can I take a look at them?"

Benny sat at the table. "They're not attractions at the zoo."

Connie joined Benny at the table. "I know that," she said. "But twins... I've never seen twins; no one has. Wizards never have twins; it's amazing. Are they special—powerful?"

Benny sighed. "Connie, please. They look like any other thirteen-year-old boy and girl, and, to answer one of your questions, yes, they are special. But that has nothing to do with their powers, which they've only just learned about and tried once." Benny glanced down the hall. "But, Maddie *did* show me something: she seems to have great control, and Jack," Benny shook his head, "He has great strength that he's going to need to get a hold of." He cleared his throat and changed the subject. "Stanton knows the situation, I assume?"

Connie nodded. "Yes. Stanton wants to follow your lead on this because of your relationship with the twins. He will offer any help the moment it's needed. Trackers have been sent out to try to locate Ray and Tina; no one

34

expects positive results. Stanton also agrees that their lives are probably not in any immediate danger."

"I don't think Tardon would do anything to hurt his chances of luring the twins to him." Benny replied.

"We aren't going to let the twins go to him, are we?"

Benny picked up a mug from the table. "At some point, we'll have no choice."

Connie leaned forward. "So, their training begins tomorrow as planned?"

Benny sipped from the mug. "Yes, but we may have to speed things up a bit. Be here bright and early."

Connie got up and started for the hallway. "No problem. Can I take a quick look at them before I go?"

Benny rolled his eyes. "Fine. Just don't wake them."

They walked down the hall, and Benny opened the door to the spare room very quietly. Connie looked over his shoulder into the room.

"How did you manage to get them to sleep with all they've been through?"

"Calming potion and a strong suggestion," Benny said as he closed the door and led the way back down the hall. "We all need to get some rest," he stated, walking to the front door.

"Bright and early?" Connie confirmed.

Benny opened the door. "Yes, and bring some good luck."

She smiled. "If the twins live up to their billing, we won't need any luck." And with that sentiment, she walked out the door into the forest.

Benny closed the door behind her, and walked back down the hall. He looked in at the twins again. "I hope everyone's not expecting too much of you," he whispered. Then he closed the door, and went to his own room across the hall.

Seven

The harsh squawking of a crow woke Jack. He tried to roll over and cover his ears, but the sound wouldn't be muffled. He opened his eyes, and the unfamiliar surroundings confused him for a moment. Then, the reality of the previous day's events jolted him to action. He leapt from the bed and bounded across the room to where Maddie was sleeping.

"Maddie," he said, shaking his sister. "Get up. Come on, get up!"

Never one to wake easily, Maddie tried to get rid of him. "Leave me alone, Jack," she said. "And get out of my room."

"I'm not in your room and neither are you. Now, get up."

Jack's words hit her like a splash of cold water and Maddie sat up. "That's right," she said. "We need to find out what happened to Mom and Dad." She quickly got out of bed and headed to the door.

"Wait," Jack said, and Maddie stopped in her tracks.

He held out his hand and the door opened as though a gust from a hurricane had blown it in. Maddie looked at her brother. "Really?" she asked in exasperation.

Jack shrugged, and they went to find Benny.

In the hall they were met by the pleasing aromas of bacon, eggs, and toast. They followed their noses and found Benny in the kitchen just finishing filling a platter with bread. He caught sight of the twins as he placed the dish on the already set dining room table.

"Good morning, you two," Benny said. "Did you sleep well?"

The twins exchanged glances, and then slid into the seats they occupied the night before. Benny placed a plate of bacon on the table and sat down. He began piling the plate from the buffet he'd set and urged the twins to do the same.

"Come on now, eat up. We've got a big day ahead of us," he told them.

Jack didn't hesitate. He filled his plate while Maddie took only a small amount.

"Does that include finding Mom and Dad?" she asked.

"There are people working on that as we speak," Benny answered. "And they will be found; but first, we have to get you two started on your training."

"Training?" Jack asked through a mouthful of eggs.

Benny picked up a piece of bread. "Absolutely," he said. "What did you think: I'd tell you were a wizard and turn you loose on the world without instruction?"

Maddie washed down a small mouthful of eggs with the juice that was in front of her plate. "Getting back to Mom and Dad," she reminded him. "Who is out looking for them?"

"Members of the guard, and Stanton," Benny said, taking a gulp of hot coffee.

Maddie looked at her brother, who, though listening kept right on eating. She tried to ignore his chewing, and leaned back in her chair. "I hate to be disrespectful," she began. "But you're going to have to tell us more than that."

Benny put his coffee cup down, wiped his mouth with a napkin, and sat back. "Okay," he replied. "Let's start at the beginning."

Jack looked up from his plate and put down his fork; he wanted to pay attention to this.

"Last night, I told you about the different realms of existence that make up the world," Benny began. "Well, those realms are meant to stay separate. Rational thought and dreams have a natural conflict, as do the magic and non-magic. If the realms co-mingle, it could mean the end of the world." Benny paused to let this sink in. He wanted the twins to fully understand, and he looked into their eyes.

Convinced that they were following along, he continued. "Wizards have debated this point for some time. Many believe that if the magical realm took over the non-magic, wizards would be able to harness the powers from the dream and thought realms and rule over all the realms, and the world. Others, like myself, your parents, and, of course, Stanton, don't agree. We believe that if dreams interfered with thought, nothing could be accomplished; the future great inventions of the world would never be possible."

Maddie interrupted. "But don't the ideas for great inventions start out as dreams?"

"An idea and a dream are not the same thing," Benny said. "Dreams take you away from reality; in a dream, you can be and do anything. An idea, even a fantastic one, has its roots in reality. It's something that is possible."

"Okay," Jack said. "I get that, but if the realms are meant to be kept separate, how do we dream and have ideas?"

Benny winked at Jack. "I'm glad you're paying attention, Jack," he said. Dreams and thoughts are, by nature, members of all the realms. They have their origin in their own realms, but find their way into the other realms to inspire. But, there are some in this realm who wish to control thoughts and dreams, in order to have people from the magic and non-magic realms follow them blindly."

"Who are these people?" Maddie asked.

"The one who took your parents," Benny answered. "The one we've been fighting for years: Tardon."

"And who is that?" Jack said.

"Tardon is a very powerful wizard who, long ago, bought into the beliefs I've just told you about. He wants to rule all the realms of existence, to influence all thoughts and dreams, and to have an army of followers who will not be able to think of act for themselves—who will have no hopes for the future," Benny said as he stood. "He has convinced a great many wizards that the magical realm must take over all the other realms. He has them believing that the separation of the realms has kept them from achieving magical greatness; that everything they've ever wanted will be theirs if they follow him. This has caused a divide in the magical realm. Stanton, a powerful wizard himself, has many who believe that the world will be doomed if the realms mingle.

"There was a great battle many years ago. The result was a divide in the magical realm, with Tardon now ruling the west and Stanton the east. Stanton and his guard, of which myself, and your parents are members, have kept Tardon from mingling the realms, but it is getting harder by the day. Your parents wanted you to be safe, so they took you from this realm, until now, when your powers will become evident."

"So, Tardon came into the non-magic realm for Mom and Dad?" Maddie asked.

"Not exactly," Benny said. "Tardon recruits the young as soon their wizarding skills begin to show. By taking your parents, he believes he will draw you to him." He paused and took a deep breath. "I am hoping that before he confronts you, you will have made the choice to be on our side."

"There is no choice," Jack said. "I will never live my life as a thoughtless follower of anyone."

"That's my brother: the great thinker." Maddie said.

"Shut up," Jack said, and pushed Maddie gently.

"Then," Benny replied. "I take it you've decided."

Maddie and Jack looked at each other. "I don't think we've made any decisions other than doing whatever we have to do to get our parents back," Maddie said.

Benny nodded. "Understood. Finish your breakfast and we'll get started on your training."

Cris Pasqueralle

Eight

After breakfast and a quick cleanup, the twins and Benny headed out into the woods. As they exited Benny's home, he knocked twice on the side of the tree, and the door vanished. Then he waved a hand across the trunk.

"You can't be too careful," he said, and motioned for the twins to follow him into the forest.

As they followed, Jack constantly looked around. He took his role as big brother seriously, even if it was only by a matter of seconds.

The forest began to thin, and they soon came to a worn path. Jack stopped, but Maddie followed Benny a little further until she realized her brother wasn't with them. She turned and saw Jack standing a few feet behind her. He was staring into the woods, and she ran to him.

"Jack, are you okay?" she asked when she reached him.

Jack pointed to a spot a few yards ahead. "What is that?" he whispered.

Just ahead of them, gnawing on the bone of some unknown dead animal, was an enormous, hairless dog.

"That's a Keelut," Benny said, walking up behind them. "And we should probably move on before it notices us."

Maddie's eyes went wide and she began to back up slowly. "I think it's too late."

The Keelut *had* noticed them. It was growling viciously and drool dangled from the corners of its mouth. As it ran toward them, Benny stepped in front of the twins and raised a hand. Before he could take any further action, a small, chubby man burst from the bushes. He whistled loudly, and the large dog ran in the opposite direction.

The small man wore a look of annoyance as he approached Benny and the twins. He was about three feet tall and had a large belly, but his arms and shoulders were thick with muscle. His head was covered with a long mane of blonde hair, and he had a long nose and pointed ears. He wore what looked like a Swiss hiking outfit complete with shorts, suspenders, and hiking boots that appeared to be twice as large as they should be for someone his height.

"Benny, you should know by now to ignore the Keelut. He won't bother you if you just go about your business."

"Good morning, Togo," Benny said. "Of course I know better, but it seems that the curiosity of my young friends got the better of them."

Togo looked at the twins and his face went blank. "Are these…"

"Ray and Tina's twins? Yes, they are," Benny interrupted. "We are about to begin their training."

Togo bowed. "Very good. You couldn't have a better mentor. Best of luck to you both," he said, and then he waved and disappeared into the forest.

"Come, we have to get to your training," Benny directed.

The twins didn't move. They stared at each other with their mouths opened slightly.

Benny clapped his hands to get their attention. "Come on now, we need to get moving."

Jack and Maddie blinked and focused on Benny.

"Who, or *what*, was that?" Jack asked.

Benny laughed as he began to walk, and the twins followed. "That is Togo."

Jack and Maddie kept looking in the direction Togo had gone as they walked with Benny.

"But, what is he?" Maddie questioned. "He's not human."

Cris Pasqueralle

"No, he's not," Benny affirmed. "He's a Forest Gnome, and son of the Gnome Chief, Rogo. He is also my protector."

Suddenly, there was a loud rustling and a thud. Benny and Maddie turned and saw Jack lying on the ground. Maddie laughed as she went back to help him. He waved her off and got back to his feet.

"Are you okay?" Maddie asked, still laughing a bit.

"Yes, I'm fine." Jack replied, slightly embarrassed. "You can stop laughing now."

"No, I really can't," Maddie said.

"Please be more careful," Benny urged, a large smile on his face.

Jack ignored their giggles. "Why do you need a protector?"

"I couldn't live in the forest if one of the Gnomes didn't agree to be my protector, and the Chief didn't give permission," Benny told them. "There is a delicate balance to nature and the Gnomes see to it that the balance isn't disturbed. They allow me to live here as long as I do not upset things. Togo makes certain that I don't."

"I don't get it," Jack replied. "What does he protect you from?"

"The other Gnomes; they don't all want me here."

"So he follows you around all the time," Jack said. "That's kind of creepy."

"No," Benny answered. "Togo can sense disturbances in the forest, and he acts accordingly. He has better things to do than to follow me around all day." He stopped walking. "This is where we will begin your training."

Cris Pasqueralle

Nine

Though they were still in the forest, before them was a field of grass surrounded by trees, as if it was a place cut off from the rest of the world. Jack's eyes fell on Connie as she walked toward them from the middle of the field. She wasn't much older than he, and as he watched her, Maddie tapped the bottom of his chin.

"Close your mouth," Maddie scolded. "You're starting to drool, and she's too old for you anyway."

Jack looked at Maddie. "What do you know?"

Connie stopped in front of the twins and looked at them for a few seconds before addressing Benny.

"So," she began. "These are our students."

"Yes," Benny confirmed. "Jack, Maddie, this is Connie: one of my finest students. She will be assisting me with your training. Contrary to what you've read in books or seen in movies, there are no real spells to bring forth your magic. Using your powers is more about believing in yourself than using words to pull things out of thin air. You have to truly want what you are asking from your powers, and you have to completely trust yourself."

51

"That doesn't sound too hard," Jack stated.

Connie responded with: "For someone with self-confidence, it shouldn't be. But, plenty of people have led difficult lives, or are shy, or have trouble trusting their instincts for whatever reason. For those people, developing their powers can be extremely difficult." She looked Jack over. "I don't think you'll have much trouble."

Jack smiled and looked at the ground. Maddie rolled her eyes. "I can see how a person could have difficulty," Maddie said.

"I have found," Benny started to say, "that the best way for a wizard-in-training to learn their strengths and weaknesses is under pressure. It is in stressful situations that we find our courage—what we are made of."

He raised a hand toward the sky, and suddenly, a dark cloud filled the sky. It was accompanied by a loud buzzing that became louder as the cloud moved closer.

"Those are locusts," Maddie pointed out.

"And they're coming right for us," Jack said, finishing his sister's thought.

The twins dropped low to the ground, thinking that they could avoid the oncoming horde of bugs, but the swarm only flew that much lower. Realizing that they wouldn't be able to duck out of the way, Jack stood. He stretched out his arm and raised his hand, like a cop directing traffic, and before they reached the twins, the insects began to fall out of the sky as if they'd hit a wall of glass. Maddie got up and she and Jack traded a high five but the bugs weren't finished yet.

The bugs quickly regrouped and took flight again. They circled high and made another run at the twins. This time, Maddie stepped forward. She put her arms out in front of her body, in the shape of a hoop, and the bugs flew right through it and were trapped in an invisible container. Maddie made a motion as if she was sealing a giant Ziplock bag with the insects inside.

Connie clapped and Benny smiled widely. "Well done," Benny commended.

The celebration was short-lived, as the wind picked up so strong, that Jack and Maddie had to lean on one another to keep from being blown over.

"Can't we take a break?" Jack yelled over the howling wind.

Benny leaned close to Connie. "Are you doing this?" he asked.

Connie shook her head.

"Then be ready for anything," he said.

53

With a loud crack, a branch from a nearby tree gave way and hit Connie on the side of the head, knocking her to the ground. She didn't move, and as Benny went to her aid, the sky went dark. He looked up at the black clouds that were gathering overhead and becoming thicker and thicker, the wind swirling them violently through the sky. In the center of the clouds, an eagle the size of a van was descending toward Jack and Maddie.

"What is that!?" Maddie yelled.

"A Thunderbird," Benny answered. "Head into the woods; it's too big to follow you."

As the twins ran toward the tree line, the giant bird went after them. It shot lightning at them from its eyes and the twins ran in a zigzag pattern to avoid the bolts. Just as they reached the trees, one lightning bolt exploded at the base of a large pine and the tree burst into flames.

The twins fell to their knees and wrapped their arms around each other. Tears ran down Maddie's cheeks, and Jack's whole body shook. The huge eagle landed a few feet in front of them and began walking toward them, its screeching causing a sharp pain in Jack and Maddie's ears.

Connie got to her feet, and she and Benny ran toward the twins who were now standing to face their attacker.

The twins held hands as the dinosaur-sized bird let out a tremendous squawk. They pulled closer together so that their heads touched. A bright, golden light emanated from the twins, and as Connie and Benny ran closer, they were forced to stop and shield their eyes.

The golden light encircled Jack and Maddie, and when the bird moved in to swallow them in its great beak, a blinding flash split the darkness and the eagle vaporized.

The wind stopped instantly, and the bright blue sky returned. The twins had fallen to the ground, and Connie began to go to them. But Benny grabbed her arm.

"This is a power I've never seen," he said. "I'll take care of them; I need you to go to Stanton and tell him what just happened. These two may be beyond my teaching skills."

Cris Pasqueralle

Ten

Connie left immediately on her assignment, and Benny hurried to check on the twins. They were sitting up now, breathing heavily, and sweating as though they were inside a pizza oven.

"Are you two all right?" Benny asked.

Jack looked at Benny, then got to his feet and helped up Maddie. "Other than almost becoming bird food, we're fine," he said.

"That was a pretty extreme lesson," Maddie managed, while still trying to catch her breath.

"That was no lesson," Benny said, looking into the sky. "I don't know how anyone knew where to send the Thunderbird, but, if you're up to it, we should get out of here."

Jack held his head in both hands and leaned over. He took several deep breaths and was able to stop himself from getting sick. He rested his hands on his knees and took several more breaths.

Maddie went over to him and put her hand on his back. "Are you okay?" she asked.

Jack didn't say anything; he simply nodded a few times to let his sister know that he was all right. Then he took in a long breath and straightened, looking at Benny. "You know," he said. "I don't think I like you so much anymore."

Maddie gasped. "Jack! How could you say that?"

"Think about what's happened to us, Maddie!" Jack yelled. "Yesterday, we were regular kids and today, are parents are gone. A Gnome—a Gnome, Maddie—saved us from some weird-looking dog, a giant bird tried to eat us," he pointed at Benny, "and it's his fault. If he didn't bring us here..."

"You would be dead," a calm, unfamiliar voice interrupted.

The twins looked in the direction of the voice. A tall, wide-shouldered man walked toward them. He was wearing a long white cloak, his face surrounded by a thick mane of red hair. As he came closer, his presence seemed to surround them. He stopped beside Benny, and the two exchanged nods, but Jack's anger had already made its way forward.

"This is great," Jack said to Maddie. "Here's another freak we have to deal with."

"I assure you," the man said. "I am no freak."

"I'm sorry," Benny said to the man.

The man patted Benny's shoulder. "No need," he said, and turned his attention to the twins. "I am Stanton, and before we go any further, I believe that Benny has suggested that we leave here. As is his habit, he has had a very good idea." He turned to Benny. "May I?"

"Please," Benny answered.

Stanton waved an arm, and in an instant, they were all in Benny's living room.

Jack looked around the room and fell into the leather recliner. "You people have to stop making us appear wherever you want."

"Pretty soon you'll be able to do it yourself," Stanton said as he casually waved his hand and the kitchen chairs moved into the living room. He sat down, and so did Maddie and Benny.

"I don't want to be able to do it," Jack argued. "I don't want to learn to move things around, and I don't want weird animals trying to kill me. I just want to go home and get back to my regular life."

"I understand you feeling a bit overwhelmed," Stanton said. "However, did you notice that you and your sister were able to save yourselves from that weird animal?"

Jack shrugged. "So? We killed it before it killed us."

Stanton leaned forward. "I noticed you said *we*."

Jack sat up and exchanged a long look with his sister.

"Yeah," Maddie confirmed. "It was both of us."

Stanton smiled at Benny. "How do you know that, Maddie?"

"Because we could feel each other's thoughts," Jack answered for her.

"You mean: hear them," Benny said.

"No," Jack said.

"That's right," Maddie explained. "It wasn't something I could hear in my head; it was something I felt, all over."

"And what did you feel?" Stanton asked.

Maddie looked at Jack. "That Jack wanted me to be safe."

"And what did *you* feel, Jack?" Stanton questioned.

"That Maddie wanted me to be safe."

"And that one, shared feeling kept both of you safe," Stanton said and then turned to Benny. "One, with the power of two."

"What does that mean?" Maddie asked, but Stanton ignored her question and addressed Jack instead.

"Jack, I truly do understand your frustration and confusion with all that's happened. However, before you decide to return to your previous life, I'd like you and Maddie to go on a rescue mission."

Maddie leapt from her seat. "To find Mom and Dad?" She grabbed Jack's arm. "Jack, you have to say yes to this," she urged.

Jack turned to Maddie. "I want to find Mom and Dad as much as you do; I just don't want to get killed doing it."

Stanton smiled. "I think," he said. "As long as you two stay together, you'll be just fine." He turned to Benny. "Benjamin, my resources into Tardon's territory are not as far reaching as your own. We have been unsuccessful in finding a trail to Tina and Ray, but I remember that you have some connections that may prove helpful."

"Yes," Benny confirmed. "But that would require a journey into the White Mountains."

"I'm certain that Rogo will be able to arrange safe passage with the Mountain Gnomes."

Benny stood. "What about the twins' training?"

"It will have to be continued as you travel; we can wait no longer. I believe that if we do, Tardon will attempt to find the twins himself. He won't be able to pinpoint where you are if you're on the move."

"I take it we are to travel by non-magical means?" Benny said.

"Yes," Stanton said. "And please try to limit the magic to training only, unless it becomes necessary to defend yourselves. Take Constance with you, and keep me informed." Stanton turned to the twins. "I will see you both very soon."

In an instant Stanton was gone. Benny went into the kitchen and knocked on the roof of the little house. Jingo, the fairy, came out immediately.

"I need Connie here, ready for travel, and I need an audience with Chief Rogo," Benny told him.

The fairy nodded, glowed brightly, and shot through the wall.

"What was that?" Maddie asked, her eyes wide.

"Wizard post office," Benny answered. "I believe a meal is in order before we set off." He began to put lunch together while Jack and Maddie simply stared at each other.

Eleven

The twins picked their way through a light lunch of fruit salad and toast that Benny had prepared for them, but their thoughts were on too many other things to focus on eating.

"Well," Benny said. "I hope you two had enough to hold you for a while; journeys into the deep forest are never easy."

"We'll be fine," Jack said. The tension in his voice wasn't missed by Benny or Maddie.

Benny looked at Jack for moment, and then he cleared the table with a wave of his hand, and walked down the hall and into his room.

Maddie slapped Jack on the arm. "Why do you have to be like that?"

Jack looked down the hall to make sure he was alone with his sister. "What should I do, Maddie? Should I act like I'm happy about all of this when I'm not? I just can't do that."

"Keep your voice down," Maddie said as she also took a peek down the hall. "I'm not saying you have to act happy, but don't act like a jerk. Stay focused on the same things I am: getting Mom and Dad back, and getting home."

Jack smiled, leaned back in his seat, and folded his arms. "I knew it," he said. "You don't want any part of this wizard crap either."

"I never said I didn't want any part of this," Maddie answered, looking down the hall again. "But our lives were a lot less dangerous a day ago."

Jack leaned forward. "Okay. So we find Mom and Dad, let them know how we feel, and we're home."

"That's what I'm hoping." Maddie agreed.

"I'll play nice then," Jack said. "But I'll only go so far."

"And how far will that be?" Maddie asked.

Jack shrugged. "I'll let you know when we get there."

A door down the hall opened, and Benny came out carrying a large duffle bag. "I hope you two are ready to go," he said as he made his way down the hall. "Connie will be here any second, and we have to get moving right away."

Jack hurried to Benny and took the large bag from him.

"Let me help you," he said, glancing at his sister. "I'm sorry I've been acting like a jerk."

Benny picked up a smaller bag. "It's fine," he said. "You've had a lot to deal with in just a short time."

They took the bag into the living where Maddie joined them. Benny removed two wool ponchos from it, and gave one to each of the twins.

"These are coated with a potion that will keep the bugs away. Some of the insects can be pretty nasty, and we don't need to deal with any bites or stings," he told them.

Suddenly, there was a loud thud outside the door, and the unhappy sounds of some kind of animal.

"You dumb beast!" a woman's voice said. "You've dropped everything."

"Our ever graceful Miss Connie has arrived," Benny said.

Jack hurried to open the door. Just outside, Connie was struggling to secure a large pack to the back of a goat. The goat was having none of it and kept moving, kicking, and hissing at Connie. Finally, she threw the pack on the ground.

"I give up," she said, and sat on top of the pack.

Benny tried to hide his laughter, but Maddie wasn't so tactful and laughed openly. Jack walked over to the goat.

"Easy boy," Jack cooed as he extended a hand under the goat's nose. The goat sniffed at him several times and Jack slowly moved his hand to the top of the goat's head and patted it gently. He moved close and put his cheek against the goat's.

"Do you think you can help us?" Jack said. "We really need you to carry our packs for us. You're the strongest and the only one we trust to do it. Will you please help us?"

The goat nodded and turned to make it easy for Jack to secure the packs.

Connie looked at Jack. "How did you do that?"

Maddie answered. "Jack's always been good with animals."

"They have feelings just like we do," Jack explained. "If you show them that you respect their feelings, they'll respect you. It's like Mom and Dad taught us. Treat others the way you want to be treated; I just apply it to animals, too."

Benny patted him on the back. "That's very smart, Jack, and something we should all remember," he said, while looking at Connie.

"Yeah, yeah," Connie griped. "Let's get going."

The twins put the ponchos on, Benny secured his home, and Connie took the rope to lead the goat. Jack stopped her.

"Maybe I should take that," he said.

"Not a bad idea," Connie agreed, and handed him the rope.

They walked in silence for a long time, Benny leading them deeper and deeper into the forest. The trees and bushes became larger and denser the more that they walked, and sticks and thorns grabbed at them at every turn. Finally, Benny stopped.

"This trip just gets better and better," Connie said as she sat under a tree.

After he tethered the goat, Jack sat beside her. Maddie made a face at Jack for sitting so close to Connie, but he paid her no attention. He'd heard Connie's disdain for Togo, and acted on it.

"Why do we need him?" Jack asked.

Benny sat on a large boulder across from Jack and Connie. "We will be traveling into the White Mountains that make up the border between the east and west territories. In order to travel safely into the mountains, we will need the permission of the Mountain Gnomes. We will ask the forest Gnome Chief to secure that permission for us, and Togo will escort us to see Chief Rogo, who is also Togo's father."

"I don't understand," Maddie said. "Can't you travel wherever you want?"

Connie smiled. "Of course we can travel where we like, but isn't it better to show respect to the people who live in the area we wish to visit?"

"And to have them offer us protection is even more of a benefit," Benny said.

"Don't you think we can protect ourselves?" Jack asked.

"Absolutely," Benny said. "But the people who live in a place that's unfamiliar to us will have a better understanding of the local dangers and how to avoid them. Also, by seeking permission and showing respect, we gain some valuable allies." He stood and looked into the distance. "Togo is nearly here."

They all got up and watched as Togo approached them. He took very long strides for someone his size, and he moved in sync with the wind that blew the leaves. As he came closer, it was apparent that even though he stirred the dirt and twigs, he made no sound as he walked. Togo was completely one with his surroundings. He called out from a few feet away.

"I hope you haven't disturbed the forest too much on your way here," he said.

Benny waited for Togo to get close before replying. "We have done our best," he said, extending a hand. They shook and Togo turned to Connie.

"Miss Connie," he said and bowed slightly. He took Connie's hand and kissed it.

Jack cleared his throat loudly, and Maddie looked at the ground so that no one would see her giggle.

Togo then turned to the twins. "My young friends. It's very nice to see you again."

"It's nice to see you, too," Maddie said, and Benny smiled at her manners.

Togo noticed the goat and went over to him. He rubbed the goat under his chin. "I hope they are treating you kindly, brother," he said, and the goat stamped its foot.

Togo turned back to Benny. "I have informed my father of the message you sent. He understands the importance of what you seek, and will be happy to intercede on your behalf. However, a vote of the table is needed for final approval. They are waiting for us."

"I had hoped this would be an informal matter," Benny said.

"As did I," Togo said. "But the table wishes to know who you are travelling with and for what purpose." He tugged on Benny's arm, and Benny bent low so that Togo could whisper in his ear. "Personally, I think they want to get a look at the twins," he said.

"I get that," Benny replied. "But we really don't have time."

Togo shrugged. "Nothing we can do, unless you wish to travel into the mountains unprotected."

Benny sighed. "Lead on, my friend. Lead on."

Twelve

The group followed Togo on a long walk, deep into the forest, where the trunks of the trees were as thick as elephant legs, and the leaves dense enough to cast the group into near darkness. After some time, Togo stopped. He put his hand against a large rock, leaned close, and appeared as if he were whispering to it. When several seconds had passed, an opening emerged and the rock became a cave entrance. Togo walked inside, picked up a lit torch that hung just inside the entrance, and waved at the group to follow him.

The second they entered the cave, Jack and Maddie were hit with smells of mold and dampness that reminded them of the time their basement had flooded. The cave turned out to be more of a large tunnel that had a downward incline, which lead them further and further underground as they continued to walk. At several points along the way, there were Gnomes who were larger than Togo. They had on the same odd hiking outfit, but held spears and wore metal helmets. They stopped the group at the entrance to a second cave. The guards looked at Togo, and dropped to one knee, bowing their heads.

Togo touched each of them on the shoulder and they rose. He then pointed to the visitors.

"These are the ones whom the table awaits," he said. The guards stepped aside, allowing Togo to lead everyone inside.

Torches hung on the walls of the interior cave, and the light they gave exposed a very large space. There were small benches carved into the walls where hundreds of Gnomes were seated. In the center of the room was a large table carved from rock, and seated around it were eleven old Gnomes. The Gnome at the head of the table stood when Togo entered. He was very old, bald, and had a very large white beard with hair growing from his ears—which matched the color of his beard.

Togo motioned for the group to follow him and they walked down a few steps to where the table was. As they passed the table, the Gnomes seated there bowed their heads at Togo. When they reached the head of the table Togo pointed to a long bench off to the side. Benny sat and the rest of the group did the same.

Togo embraced the old Gnome and then knelt before him. He kept his head bowed as he spoke. "Chief Rogo," he began, and then paused. "Father, these wizards come to ask that you speak to the Chief of our cousins, the

72

Mountain Gnomes, in order to secure them permission to travel into The White Mountains."

Chief Rogo tapped Togo on the shoulder. "Take your seat," he commanded.

Togo rose, waited for the Chief to take his seat, and then took the empty seat beside his father.

"Benny," Chief Rogo said. "Come forward."
Benny stood, walked before the table, and nodded a greeting that was returned by all those at the table.

"Tell us," Rogo said. "Why do you wish to travel into The White Mountains?"

Benny bowed. "Friends of mine have been taken captive, and there is someone I know in the mountains who may be able to help us."

The Chief leaned forward. "Who has taken your friends?"

Benny looked around the room. "Tardon."

There was a gasp from the spectators, and they began to chatter among themselves.

"There will be silence!" Rogo yelled, and banged his hand on the table. The room immediately became quiet. Rogo sighed. "Who are the captives?"

"Ray and Tina," Benny answered. "Parents of the twins."

Rogo looked around the room as if he expected another outburst, but his authority kept the room quiet.

A female Gnome seated at the opposite head of the table raised her hand.

"Fala," Rogo said, somewhat surprised. "Do you wish to speak?"

"If I may," she said, and rose from her seat.

Like Rogo, Fala was very old and she was wearing something that looked like a dress worn by peasants in the fairy tale books. She had long gray hair that was braided, and she smiled a very friendly smile that seemed to welcome everyone.

Rogo held out a hand toward her, and Fala spoke. "It appears that this is a matter between wizards. For us to ask our cousins in the mountains to offer protection would be dragging us into something that is none of our concern. There is nothing to prevent them from traveling into the mountains on their own, and I'm sure they can protect themselves. I see no reason for us to get involved in a struggle between Tardon and Stanton."

Togo stood. "May I, Father?" he asked.

Rogo made a gesture that Togo had the floor, and Togo faced Fala. "Mother," he said. "I know that you wish for us to remain apart from the wizards, but that has become impossible, as their struggle has become ours. Tardon and his followers travel where they wish, without regard for those who live in these places. They have turned many free creatures into slaves and set them to evil tasks. Now, Tardon has taken the parents of the ones who can free us from this menace, and you say we should not get involved. Mother, we are involved, and we should offer this protection to make their struggle easier."

Rogo nodded at Togo, and Togo sat. "Does anyone else wish to speak?" Rogo questioned.

Maddie took Jack's hand, and they stood. They walked before Rogo, and the crowd gasped once more. Rogo held up a hand and there was immediate silence. "Do you wish to say something?" he asked.

Maddie's legs shook slightly, and she cleared her throat to find her voice. "Y-Yes, sir," she said.

"Very well, you may speak," Rogo permitted.

"I don't know anything about taking sides," Maddie began. "And I don't know who gives permission to travel where, but I do know that Uncle Benny knows someone who can help us find our parents, and if you can help us get to that person, I wish you would. We miss our parents and we want them back."

75

Rogo stood and walked over to Maddie. He patted her on the shoulder and smiled. Then he held out his arms to those seated around the table. "Can we have a vote?" he asked. "All in favor?" Eight of the Gnomes around the table raised their hands. "Against?" The remaining four Gnomes raised their hands. "Very well," Rogo said. "I will send a message to the Mountain Chief, and in the morning, Togo will guide you to the border."

Thirteen

After the meeting, Togo and his parents led the twins, Benny, and Connie to a smaller cave a few feet from the meeting room. There was an animal skin hanging from the entrance that acted as the door, and when they went inside, Jack and Maddie felt as if they had entered a real-life version of the Flintstones.

There was a stone table in the center of the room with two stone benches on either side of it. In a corner was a small opening carved in the wall where a fire was lit, and a large mettle pot was hanging over it. Animal skins hung on the walls, and several large boulders were placed about to serve as extra chairs.

Fala went over to the fire and stirred the contents of the pot with a large wooden spoon. Whatever was in the pot filled the cave with a scent that was both sweet and sour, and was not at all unpleasant. Togo went over to his mother and began handing her wooden bowls, which she filled from the pot, and Togo placed them on the table. Rogo motioned for everyone to sit. He sat on a large boulder at the head of the table. Togo, Fala, and

Benny sat on the bench to his left, and the twins and Connie sat on the bench to Rogo's right.

Rogo bowed his head and when Togo and Fala did the same, the rest of the group followed.

"We thank you, Mother Nature, for providing us with this sustenance and for granting us the great privilege to live among your bounty. Please watch over our friends in their quest to reunite their family." Rogo looked up. "Please," he said. "Everyone eat."

Jack and Maddie exchanged a quick glance before looking into their bowls and being happily surprised to find it contained a clear vegetable soup. With their fear of having to eat something strange gone, the twins remembered how hungry they were and picked up their wooden spoons and dug in. The soup tasted exactly the way it smelled, sweet and sour, and very good.

Benny cleared his throat. "Chief Rogo," he began. "I mean no disrespect, but I really don't think it necessary for Togo to escort us to the White Mountains. A word from you should be enough for the Mountain Gnomes to allow our passage."

"Togo must go," Rogo said. "He is your sworn protector in these woods, and also in your dealings with any Gnomes. It is his duty to make the introductions."

"I understand that," Benny said. "But you must understand that it is possible that Tardon knows we are traveling, and may make an attempt to impede our progress."

Jack dropped his spoon, and Maddie choked on a mouthful of soup.

"What?!" Jack exclaimed, while Maddie coughed. He looked at his sister and slapped her back a few times until she stopped.

Maddie cleared her throat loudly and took a sip of water. "How can Tardon know where we are?" Maddie asked.

"How did he know where to send the Thunderbird?" Connie questioned.

Benny put up his hands to stop the onslaught of questions. "Okay. Let's get this out right now. Tardon is no fool. He must be expecting you to come looking for your parents, and he also wants to test your strength so he knows what he's dealing with. So, he sent a Thunderbird to test you, and I'm sure he's not finished sending you challenges"

Jack stood. "And when were you planning to tell us this?"

Maddie touched Jack's hand. He took a long, calming, breath, and sat down.

"We never expected this to be easy," Maddie said. "But we would like to know what we need to be prepared for, and how to be prepared."

"We're not stopping your training," Connie said. "Benny and I have a whole series of lessons designed to teach you to defend yourselves. Trust us."

Jack addressed Maddie. "Can you believe this? They don't tell us our lives could be in danger, and they want us to trust them."

Maddie rubbed Jack's shoulder, trying to keep him from exploding. "We would appreciate it if you kept us better informed."

Benny understood. "Okay. I guess you two are more grown up than I thought."

"Not to change the subject," Fala interjected. "But am I to understand that you expect danger before you even reach the White Mountains?"

"It's possible," Benny said.

Fala looked at her son and then at Rogo.

"If you're concerned for Togo's safety, I've already said that he does not need to escort us," Benny reminded her.

"Of course I'm concerned for his safety," Fala said. "He is my son."

"Then he can stay," Benny said.

"That is impossible," Rogo argued. "The promise has been made."

"That's true," Togo agreed. "But I don't believe that Mother is suggesting that I don't go; I believe she'll be coming with us."

"That can't happen," Benny protested. "I cannot put anymore of you in danger." He turned to Rogo. "Chief, you must not allow this."

Rogo laughed. "I am Chief of this tribe and I have power over many things. But, just like any husband, I have no power to allow or disallow my wife to do anything." He looked at Fala, who smiled at him. "Her mind is made up," he declared.

Benny looked at Fala, and she sat back and folded her arms. "Fine," he agreed.

Cris Pasqueralle

Fourteen

After agreeing to expand their traveling party, and eating a hearty meal, the twins, Connie, and Benny were led to another small cave that would serve as their sleeping quarters. There was a fire pit in the center that kept the cave warm, and in the walls were several cut outs that would be fine for Gnomes to sleep in, but not for humans. Instead, they rolled out sleeping bags that Benny had packed and placed them close to the fire. It had been a long and emotionally draining day and once everyone was spread out, the twins fell asleep within minutes.

Benny looked over at them. He was convinced they were asleep and motioned for Connie to get up. They went over to a corner of the cave and Benny whispered, "During our travels, I want you to separate the twins for their lessons. We know how strong they are together, but we have to find out what individual strengths they have."

Connie tried to clarify things. "Okay. But we're still sticking to defense."

"Yes," Benny agreed. "Learning how to protect themselves has to take priority right now; everything else will have to be taught on the fly, so to speak."

"Not ideal," Connie sighed. "But we do what we have to do."

Benny smiled. "Let's get some rest; we have some big things coming our way."

They returned to their sleeping bags and, like the twins, fell asleep quickly.

Early the next morning, they were awakened by Togo and brought back to his family cave for a breakfast of fruits, nuts, berries, and fresh baked bread. When they finished, and were ready to go, Chief Rogo led his family and the group of wizards to the entrance of the main cave. He offered Benny his hand, and Benny shook it.

"May our Mother Nature be with you and protect you," Rogo said.

Benny bowed slightly. "Thank you for everything."

"I'm always happy to help a friend. Togo has the message for our mountain cousins; I'm sure they'll allow you free passage."

Before Benny could thank him further, Rogo turned to his son. "Togo, you know your responsibility to

Benny. Lead him to the White Mountains safely, greet our kind warmly, and return quickly."

"Yes, Father," Togo said as he embraced Rogo.

Rogo then turned to Fala. "You know our son will be fine," he said.

"I do," Fala answered. "But I'm his mother and…."

"A mother must keep her children safe," Rogo finished for her. He hugged his wife, and whispered. "Come home to me soon, my love. I will count the seconds we are apart."

Connie untied the pack goat, and handed the rope to Jack. "Here," she said. "He responds to you better."

Jack took the rope and smiled. Togo and Fala slipped on their backpacks, and moved to the front to lead the way.

With the morning mist hovering around the bushes, and the early morning light streaming through the treetops, the forest had a spiritual feel that seemed to give the group energy. But, each bouncy step they took left a track in the dew-ridden earth that Benny, taking up the rear, made vanish with a wave of his hand.

He called ahead. "Jack, let me lead the goat for a while."

Jack stopped for Benny to catch up.

"I need you to talk to Connie," Benny said, and took the rope from Jack.

Jack and Connie fell back from the group but remained close enough to offer aid, or be aided, if trouble presented itself. Jack looked at Maddie as she walked ahead, beside Fala. He hesitated.

"Come on, Jack," Connie said. "This is just a talk between you and me."

Jack smiled. "Okay," he said, not minding in the least to be spending time alone with Connie. He took a deep breath. Among the morning dew, the fresh pine, and the musk of the forest, Jack detected a hint of lemon that could only be coming from Connie. She was dressed like any typical hiker: a long sleeve T-shirt to keep bugs and twigs at bay, jeans to protect her legs from low lying branches, and sturdy boots for any obstacle that might come under foot. *But she wears it all so beautifully*, Jack thought.

"Come on, Jack," Connie urged. "Let's keep walking."

Jack hadn't even realized he'd stopped. He looked ahead to see that the rest of the group was a fair distance in front, and quickened his steps.

"No," Connie said. "We're good here. Benny can still see us and we can see him."

"Okay," Jack said, and he slowed down and walked beside Connie. "What will it be today? Moving rocks out of our way, making trees bend to our will... what you got?"

Connie giggled. "You're very funny," she said. "But this lesson doesn't require any magic; we're just going to talk."

Jack shook his head. "I'm not sure a nice talk will help find my parents, but sure—why not? What's our topic?"

"Emotions," Connie said.

"Then this lesson is over," Jack said. "I have plenty of those."

Connie smiled again. "I know. That's the problem."

"I thought having emotions was a good thing?"

"It is a good thing," Connie replied. "But when you can't control them, it can become a very big problem. When the Thunderbird attacked you, fear served you well, but only because it was fear for your sister and not yourself. Fear, anger, and magic do not mix well. Even the need to protect another can cause you to make a mistake. Your emotions can alter your decisions and cause you to rush into dangerous situations without knowing what you're getting into."

Jack looked at the ground. "You sound like my Dad," he said.

"So you've heard this before?"

"More than once," Jack grumbled.

Connie put her hand on Jack's shoulder and they stopped walking. "Jack," she said, looking into his eyes. "This is very important. You have to be able to keep your head in the most stressful of times. Your emotions will always come through in the magic you perform but that magic must be guided by sound, rational, decisions. Do you understand?"

Jack fought the urge to get lost in the dark pools of Connie's eyes, and remained focused on her words. "I get it," he said. "I really do."

Connie looked at him for another second. "Okay," she said. "That's enough for now. Let's catch up to the others before Benny gets attached to that goat."

Fifteen

While Jack was getting a lesson from his favorite teacher, Maddie decided to do some investigative work. She walked quickly until she caught up to Fala, and then backed off slightly so that she was just a step behind. After a while, Fala noticed her.

"Good morning, Miss Maddie," Fala said. "I see you're keeping up just fine."

"Were you worried that I wouldn't?" Maddie asked as she moved beside Fala.

"Well, sometimes those who aren't used to walking through the forest can have a problem," Fala said as she looked Maddie over. "But it seems that Benny has outfitted you correctly…"

Before Fala could continue her critique, Maddie interrupted. "You don't approve of us, do you?"

Fala lowered her head. "I don't know you well enough to approve or disapprove."

"That's not what I mean," Maddie said.

Fala stopped. "I know what you mean," she said. "And since you wish to push the question, I will give you an answer. No. I do not approve of you coming into the forest, disturbing the lives of my people, and getting us involved in something that is none of our concern."

"The way I understand it," Maddie began. "Is that what Tardon is trying to do should be the concern of everyone. Uncle Benny said that Tardon wants to mix the realms of existence, he wants to rule over everything and everyone, and if the realms become mixed, it would upset the balance of the world and we could all die."

Fala shrugged. "That's one way of looking at it," she said, and began to walk again.

"Is there another way? Because, if I have things wrong, I'd like to know about it," Maddie said, as she stepped over some thick roots to keep up with Fala.

"I don't believe the realms can be mixed," Fala answered. "And I think this is a battle between wizards, over power, and nothing more—just egos fighting, and hurting the innocent along the way."

"But you're wrong," Maddie argued. "The realms can be mixed. I come from the non-magical realm."

Fala stopped again. "But you're a wizard; you come from magic. You can't live in the non-magical realm."

"I can and I do," Maddie said. "My parents, my brother, and I all live in the non-magical realm. Even Uncle Benny spends a lot of time with us."

Fala glanced at Benny then looked back at Maddie. "But he lives in our forest," she said, almost to herself.

"I've recently found that out," Maddie informed her. "But he's at our house almost every day."

Fala scratched her head. "So you're saying that it's possible for wizards to travel between the realms?"

Maddie shrugged. "I'm new to all of this," she said. "But what I'm telling you is true, so I guess the answer is yes."

Fala began walking again. "That still makes no difference to me and my people. You've traveled between the realms and caused no danger to anyone; I don't see how Tardon could destroy everything by doing exactly what you've already done."

"I won't pretend I understand any of this," Maddie said. "I just don't know how you can't get involved. Togo has already said that Tardon is corrupting the animals your people protect. Don't you think that soon he'll come after your people?"

Fala looked down, sighed, and then looked at Maddie. "You make a good point, young one."

Maddie smiled. "Then you'll help us?"

"I didn't say that," Fala said. "You just tell a different version of things. I must see for myself that what you say is true before I get involved in a conflict between wizards. For now, I am only here to see that my son is safe."

"And I'm only here to find my parents," Maddie said. "Maybe we can figure the rest out together."

"Maybe," Fala said, and she looked straight ahead and continued walking.

Sixteen

Jack and Connie caught up to the group and Jack took over leading the goat from Benny.

"Did you and Connie have a good talk?" Benny asked.

"I guess," Jack replied.

"Connie's one of the best students I've ever had," Benny said. "Anything she's told you will be very useful—of that I am sure."

"So you've been teaching her for a long time?" Jack asked.

"Only two years," Benny answered. "But she grasps things very quickly, and she's far ahead of where someone her age would normally be."

"Two years," Jack said, almost to himself and smiled. "That means she's only fifteen."

Benny looked at Jack as if he could see the wheels spinning in his head. "Take it easy, Jack," he warned. "Let's take on one challenge at a time."

Jack's face went red and he looked at the ground. "Did I say that out loud?"

"Don't worry," Benny said. "It'll be our secret." He laughed, and slowed to allow Connie to catch up with him.

Jack rubbed the goat's chin and whispered, "You keep it a secret, too." He could have sworn he saw the goat smile.

"So, goat boy," Maddie said as she walked next to her brother. "What's the big secret with Connie?"

Jack gasped slightly. "What did Benny tell you?" he asked.

"What are you getting so excited for?" Maddie questioned, and she looked over at Connie and then at Jack with a big smile on her face. "Is there a secret with Connie?"

Jack looked straight ahead and kept walking. "Shut up, Maddie."

Maddie stopped smiling. "Okay," she said. "What did Connie teach you?"

"Nothing," Jack said. "We just talked."

"About what?" Maddie pressed, as she pet the goat.

Jack sighed. "Apparently I let my emotions get in the way, and I should control them because emotions and magic don't mix."

"That makes sense," Maddie said.

"I know," Jack agreed. "But I don't need someone who barely knows me, telling me I have no self-control. It's hard to control how I feel."

"No one can control how they feel," Maddie said. "You can only control what those feelings make you do. It's like when basketball players 'trash talk.' They want the players on the other team to get mad and make mistakes; I guess Connie's just trying to say that it's the same with magic."

"I'm not stupid, Maddie," Jack grumbled. "I know what she's trying to say. It's just…"

"You don't want the girl you like telling you what's wrong with you," Maddie finished for him.

Jack looked at his feet and kicked at some leaves. "Sometimes, I really wish I was an only child," he mumbled.

Maddie pushed him. "I love you too, big brother."

The group moved through a row of saplings and onto a circular clearing. Togo and Fala stopped walking and put down their backpacks. Nearby was a small stream and the goat pulled Jack toward it. Jack tied the goat to a thick bush, close to the water, so he could drink his fill. The grass in the clearing was matted down as if something large had recently slept there.

Fala removed what appeared to be two large drumsticks from her pack. She walked around banging the two sticks together every few steps. Togo took several loaves of bread from his pack, and began placing them under the surrounding trees. Then he hung small pieces of metal from some of the branches.

Maddie turned to Benny. "What are they doing?" she asked.

"They're letting the Sasquatch know we're in their neighborhood," he said.

"You mean: Bigfoot is *real*?" Jack asked.

"The term 'Bigfoot' is an insult and offensive to me," Fala said.

"I'm sorry," Jack apologized. "I didn't mean it like that."

Fala sighed. "I realize that," she said. "Just don't use that term again."

"I won't; I promise," Jack said. "Can you tell me why you're doing all this?"

Togo finished tying the last string and turned to Jack. "The stick banging alerts the Sasquatch to our presence. The last thing you want to do is have a Sasquatch find you in his territory by accident."

Maddie nodded. "I can understand that," she said.

Fala continued Togo's explanation. "The metal tells the Sasquatch exactly where we are so they can avoid us if they wish. The bread is a thank you for letting us share their space."

Togo sat down beneath one of the trees. "We'll rest here for a bit," he announced.

Benny sat down as well. "Sounds good to me," he said. He opened his pack, took out several large apples, gave one to everyone, took a bite from his, and leaned back and closed his eyes.

Jack broke off a piece of his apple and brought it to the goat, which was still drinking from the stream. He patted the goat on the head and returned to the clearing where he stretched out under a large pine tree. Maddie sat beside him, but before she could get comfortable, Connie came over.

"Hi, Maddie," Connie said. "Why don't we take a walk?"

Maddie looked at her brother and Jack smiled. "Your turn, Sis," he said.

Maddie got up, and she and Connie walked into the woods by the stream, being careful to stay just far enough away for privacy, and just close enough to everyone in case there was danger.

"I'm guessing that Jack told you about our talk," Connie said.

"Yes, he did," Maddie confirmed. "I hope that's okay."

Connie smiled. "Of course that's okay; I wouldn't expect him to keep anything from you."

"Good," Maddie said. "Because he really can't keep secrets from me. Even when he tries, I always know."

Connie sat down at the edge of the stream. "It's nice that you're so close," she said.

Maddie sat down beside her. "We're twins; we have a connection."

"What's that like?" Connie asked.

Maddie scratched her head and hesitated for a second. "Well," she said. "Sometimes I can feel what he feels, and we know each other's thoughts without having to say anything. It sounds kind of weird when I say that out loud."

"I don't think that's weird at all," Connie said. "But is that something that happens all the time?"

"Now that I think about it," Maddie said. "No, it's usually when we need each other, like when something's bothering one of us."

"Like what happened with the Thunderbird," Connie commented.

Maddie leaned back, and her eyes got big. "Nothing like that ever happened before."

"I wouldn't think so," Connie said. "So, Jack told you that Benny and I think he needs to learn to control his emotions?"

Maddie nodded. "He told me that you would like him to control his emotions."

Connie looked at Maddie for several seconds, as though she were trying to read her mind. "You don't agree?"

Maddie let out a small laugh. "I wouldn't say that," she said. "Jack could do with a little control; he can lose it really quickly."

"So then, you do agree?" Connie asked.

"Not exactly," Maddie said.

"You don't think his lack of control over his emotions is a problem?"

"I guess it can be," Maddie said. "But Jack gets these gut feelings sometimes and he just acts on them, and he's usually right."

Connie pondered this for a moment. "I understand. Acting on instinct can be a good thing, but taking a second to think things through can keep you from making fatal mistakes."

Maddie laughed again. "Jack's not real big on thinking."

"You don't have that problem, though," Connie said.

Maddie lowered her eyes. "No," she said. "I'm the reasonable one."

Connie touched Maddie's hand and Maddie looked up at her. "Are you embarrassed by that?" Connie asked. "You shouldn't be. It means you're careful, and you think things through. That's what your brother needs to learn." She paused. "You two are very different."

"That's why we get along so well, most of the time," Maddie said.

Connie's eyebrows moved close together and she scratched her head. "I don't understand."

Maddie tried to explain. "I'm the things Jack isn't, and he's what I'm not; together we're whole."

"That's a very interesting way to look at it."

Maddie shrugged. "I guess."

Connie stood. "Shall we have a lesson?"

Maddie got up while Connie looked around for a few seconds. "I've got it," she said. "We often encounter obstacles that we can't easily remove, such as a river or a mountain…"

"Or a stream?" Maddie asked.

Connie laughed. "So you get the idea?"

"I think so," Maddie said.

"Okay then. Pretend this stream is a raging river. You can't walk or swim across it and there is no bridge. Without damaging your surroundings, I want you to find a way across it."

Maddie looked around. "So, I can't just make a tree fall and walk across?"

Connie shook her head. "That would be damaging your surroundings."

Maddie nodded. "Okay. Let me just think for a second."

She sat down again and stared across the stream. Within a few seconds, a white light began to radiate from Maddie and an image of her, almost ghost-like, stood up, but Maddie was still sitting. The image of Maddie floated across the stream and when it reached the other side, it turned, floated back, and rejoined the real Maddie still sitting by the water's edge. The white light faded and Maddie looked around.

"Why am I still here?" she questioned. "I know I just went across the stream."

Connie looked at Maddie with her hand over her mouth. She took a deep breath. "You did go across the stream," Connie said. "But not the way I thought."

Maddie stood, looked across the stream again, and then back at Connie. "What just happened?"

"Something very rare," Connie answered. "Very few wizards can self-project, and that's only after years of training, but you just did it, and it was amazing."

"Self-project," Maddie said. "What is that?"

"It's a way of putting yourself someplace else for a short period of time," Connie replied. "You're not really there, but you can see and hear things, and, at an advanced level, you can send messages. It can be a very useful piece of magic."

"And I just did that?" Maddie asked.

Connie gave Maddie a small hug. "Yes you did. Come on, Benny's going to want to hear about this."

Seventeen

Jack was sitting beneath a tree, his back against it and his eyes closed. Maddie ran over to where he was and fell down beside him. Jack jumped slightly and opened his eyes. He looked around and realized it was his sister who had jolted him.

"Maddie," Jack said. "Is everything okay?"

Maddie could hardly contain her smile. "Everything's great," she replied.

Jack looked around and saw Connie talking to Benny. Then he looked back at Maddie. "Did Connie give you a talking to, like me?"

Maddie shook her head. "Not exactly," she said, still smiling.

Jack straightened up. "You look very happy with yourself; what happened?"

Maddie seemed to be waiting for the question and her answer came out very fast. "We were sitting by the stream, and Connie asked me to find a way across without damaging anything and—" she realized the speed of her words and took a deep breath to slow herself down.

"While I was thinking about how to get across, Connie said I self-projected to the other side."

Jack put both hands on his sister's shoulders. "Maddie," he said. "Slow down."

Maddie took a few more breaths and seemed to settle down a little.

"Now," Jack said. "*What* did you do?"

"Self-projected," Benny interjected as he and Connie came to sit with the twins beneath the tree.

"What does that mean?" Jack asked, his eyes focused on Connie.

"To put it simply," Benny began to explain. "Maddie is able to make an image of herself go where she wants to go without actually going there."

Jack shook his head. "Yeah. That's simple."

Connie smiled. "It might be better if we just show you," she said as she stood. "Come on, Maddie; let's try it again."

Maddie leaned against the tree and looked to the other side of the clearing. This time, she closed her eyes. Within a few seconds she began to glow white.

Jack jumped up. "Is she okay?" he asked, sounding concerned.

"She's fine," Benny said as he stood too.

The ghost-like image of Maddie stepped forward from the real Maddie, walked across the clearing, and sat down beneath a small oak tree.

Benny looked on with his mouth slightly opened. "Okay," he called. "That'll do."

Maddie opened her eyes and the image vanished. She leapt to her feet. "What do you think, Jack?"

Jack had a big smile on his face. "We could mess with a lot of people with that," he said.

Maddie laughed. "Yeah, we could really have fun with this."

Benny laughed. "Always the trouble makers," he teased. "I was thinking this could be a very useful tool to gather information."

Maddie's smile faded. "Oh yeah," she said thoughtfully. "We could do that, too." Benny patted her on the back.

"Jack," he said. "Come with us."

Jack looked at Maddie and shrugged before following Benny and Connie back to the stream where Maddie had her lesson.

"Now," Benny said. "I don't expect *you* to be able to self-project; one person is rare enough. But to have two in the same family with that power would be exceptional.

All I want you to do is to find a way across the stream, using your own power, and without damaging anything around you."

"Okay," Jack said. He looked around at the things nearest him and then across the stream. It never occurred to him to sit down and concentrate on getting to the other side. Instead, Jack took action. He backed up several steps, took a deep breath, and ran at the stream as hard as he could. When he reached the edge of the water, Jack pushed off the ground hard and took to the air. He didn't leap as much as float across, and he landed perfectly on the other side. He turned around and looked at Benny and Connie. They were both staring at him with their mouths open.

"I'm across!" Jack called.

Benny and Connie looked at each other. "This is extraordinary!" Benny exclaimed.

Connie's eyes were focused on the spot where she saw Jack take flight. "I thought flyers were just a myth," she gasped.

"Flyers and self-projectors are very rare," Benny said. "It's a power that comes from within; it isn't something we can teach, and it comes only to the strongest of wizards. Send a message to Stanton; let him know what we saw. Tell him that the twins are exactly what we expected—maybe more."

Cris Pasqueralle

Eighteen

Jack ran back to Maddie to tell her about his new power. Benny and Connie followed, and Benny immediately noticed that Togo and Fala were standing with their backpacks on.

"Are we ready to get going?" Benny asked.

Togo answered. "I believe that if we keep moving without any breaks we can reach the edge of the White Mountains by dusk."

"Very good," Benny said. "I'll get everyone together so we can get moving."

Connie joined the group and was once again leading the goat. "It looked like we were ready to go, so I brought our friend," she said and looked at Benny. "I've sent the message."

Benny smiled. "I think Stanton will be pleased," he said and then called to the twins. "We're getting underway; are you two ready?"

"Whenever you are!" Maddie called back.

"Let's get moving then, shall we?" Togo asked as he moved to the lead.

The group moved quickly out of the clearing, and was soon back to pushing their way through dense bushes, ducking low-lying branches, and jumping over roots and rocks on their way through the forest. Jack had taken the goat from Connie, and she fell back to walk beside Benny. Jack and Maddie stayed just behind Togo and Fala.

"Connie said that self-projecting is very rare and that it takes a lot of practice, but I was able to do it, and I didn't even know what I was doing," Maddie said as she practically skipped through the forest.

"Maddie," Jack said. "Let's remember what we talked about. We're getting Mom and Dad and then we're going home."

Maddie sighed. "I know. But you have to admit: having these powers is pretty cool."

"You think so?" Jack asked. "We've only been here for a couple of days, and already we have to learn to defend ourselves from who knows what, we've almost been killed once, and we don't even know what else is waiting for us. You might think that our powers are cool, but I just want my regular life back. And as soon as we find Mom and Dad, I'm gone."

"Jack," Maddie said. "I know how you feel and I want to go back to being normal again too, I really do, but what if…" she stopped talking.

Jack looked around, wondering if something else was about to attack them, but things looked okay. "What is it Maddie?" he pressed.

"Well," she said. "This is where Mom and Dad are from; what if they don't want to go back?"

Jack stared at his sister. "Don't even say that. Don't even think it," he said and sighed. "They'll want to go home; they have to."

Maddie nodded to soothe her brother's concerns, but she still wondered what he would do if the family wanted to stay.

At the back of the group, Connie and Benny moved slowly.

"You think the twins are the real thing?" Connie asked.

"I've thought they were special for some time," Benny said. "Even before their powers became evident. But now, seeing what they can do with nearly no training…" Benny looked at the twins for a moment. "I have to say, I am becoming convinced."

"Well," Connie said. "If they're going to play a part in their parents' recue, they'll need to be more than special."

"Yes," Benny replied. "And since Togo wants us to keep moving, I think we should take them separately and continue their lessons."

"Okay," Connie said. "I think Jack could use a woman's touch, so I'll take him."

"I think that will make him very happy," Benny said and he looked at Connie, who had a small smile on her face. "Perhaps it makes you happy as well?" he asked.

Before Connie could answer, they were joined by Fala. "Benny, I was hoping we could talk," she said, and looked at Connie.

"I'll get started with Jack's lessons," Connie said, and quickened her pace to catch up to the twins.

Benny bowed to Fala. "What can a humble wizard do for you?"

Fala returned the bow. "I've spoken with the girl…"

"Maddie," Benny said.

"Yes," Fala confirmed. "She tells me that you travel between the magic and non-magic realms frequently."

"That's true," Benny said.

"And you cause no harm to either realm?"

Benny smiled slightly. "I see," he said. "You're wondering how it is that Tardon can cause the damage we foresee if I can move among the realms without disturbing things."

Fala bowed again. "That was my question," she said.

"Moving among the realms is one thing," Benny explained. "Attempting to influence them is quite another. If Tardon brings magic into the open, in the non-magic realm, it will distort reality for those who live there. From there, thoughts and ideas will also become distorted, then hope, ambition, desires—all will disappear and all the realms of existence with them." Benny stopped. "Tardon is playing a very dangerous game and he must be stopped, here and now."

"But," Fala said. "If wizards can move between realms, what is stopping Tardon from trying to take over right now?"

"Tardon has moved between the realms. That's how he managed to capture Ray and Tina," Benny said. "But to take control of all the realms, he must first conquer this one. And for that, he needs an army—one he is building, though Stanton has made it difficult for him. His strength is growing and so is the number of his followers. We must stop him before he obtains the force he needs."

"You paint a very disturbing picture," Fala said.

"You're right," Benny said. "It is disturbing. That's why we need all the help we can get. Will you help us?"

Falal stared at Benny for a moment. "Perhaps, but I wonder why have you not presented this to us before?"

"Stanton believes that all those in our realm must decide for themselves whether or not to take up the fight. I do apologize; it is my fault that the facts were never properly presented to you and your people."

Fala looked ahead at the twins. "Maybe the *destined ones* should present the facts," she said.

Benny smiled. "You may be right."

Nineteen

After speaking with Fala, Benny took Maddie aside and was showing her how to produce a shield of protection, when a bright, yellow light shot right between them. It circled twice and then hovered over a nearby rock. Slowly, the light dimmed away to nothing, revealing a very thin man who was only a few inches in height. He wore a blue toga and had large butterfly-like wings. He bowed before Benny.

Benny approached the tiny man, while Maddie just looked at him with her mouth opened slightly and her eyes wide.

"Mindo," Benny said. "I'm assuming you have a message from Stanton."

In a low, but squeaky voice, Mindo answered, "Yes. He says to thank you for the update; it is nothing less than he expected. Stanton also urges you to send a message to your friend in the west, as he believes Tardon is awaiting your arrival and will be prepared."

Benny sat on a fallen log that was nearby. "This is very disturbing," he said. "Thank you, Mindo; there is no reply."

Mindo bowed, and then glowed brightly once more before shooting off the same way he came.

Maddie watched as the bright light disappeared into the forest, and she looked at Benny. His face showed great concern, and he was mumbling to himself. Maddie sat beside him, but Benny didn't notice.

"How does he know we're looking for him? This is not good," he said as he banged his fist against his leg several times.

Maddie cleared her throat, and Benny finally looked at her. "Maddie," he said. "I almost forgot you were here."

"I didn't mean to interrupt you," Maddie said. "But we're being left behind."

Benny stood and looked ahead. The rest of the group had indeed walked far ahead. Benny put his pinkies in his mouth and let out a high pitched whistle that echoed through the trees. The group stopped.

"Do you mind if we catch up?" he called, and he and Maddie began a quick trot toward the others.

Togo met them. "Benny," he said. "It's very important that we keep moving if we are to reach the White Mountains before dark."

"I realize that," Benny said. "But there has been a development that we need to discuss."

Connie had walked over to Togo and Benny, and she looked at Benny. She read the worry on his face. "He knows we're coming," she guessed.

"Yes," Benny confirmed, and Fala and Jack joined the group. "It seems that the idea of travelling non-magically hasn't given us the protection we'd hoped. I will be transporting us to the base of the mountains, and we'll make camp there until we can meet with the Mountain Gnomes."

"They are expecting us in the morning; I'm sure they will be waiting," Fala said.

"Good." Benny turned to Connie. "I will send a message to Gavin." He paused and took a deep breath before addressing the twins. "I'm sorry. I never wanted your introduction to our world to be so sudden but…"

"It is what it is," Jack interrupted. "No use being upset about it now. Let's just get Mom and Dad."

Benny smirked. "It is what it is," he repeated and patted Jack on the back. "That certainly sums things up." He looked around. "Okay then. Let's get started." He clapped his hands together three times and another bright ball of light shot through the forest, landing beside him. When it dimmed, Jingo was standing next to Benny.

"I need you to go to Gavin and tell him that we've been discovered, and we will be camped nearby shortly. Tell him to prepare to meet us and to be extremely careful."

The little winged man bowed and was gone in a flash of light.

"Excuse me," Maddie said. "What was that?"

"A fairy," Connie informed her. "That's how wizards send text messages."

Twenty

While Connie made sure the twins were ready and removed the packs from the goat, Benny took Togo and Fala aside.

"I want to thank both of you for all of your help," Benny said. "But there is no reason for you to continue on with us."

Togo bowed. "You are wrong, my friend. It is my duty to introduce you to our mountain cousins and..." He paused to look at his mother before continuing. "I wish to join the fight against Tardon."

"Togo!" Fala said sternly. "That decision has not been made by the table."

Togo sighed. "No, Mother, it hasn't," he said. "But I have made it for myself. I do not speak for the tribe. I have seen the corruption of the innocent creatures of our world. Tardon and those who follow him bend the will of our brothers so they will carry out their evil deeds. This is a sin against our Great Mother and should not be tolerated. I also believe that Stanton is correct. Tardon is tampering with the harmony of the world, and this will cause damage—perhaps permanently. I feel I must do what I can to aid those who fight against him."

Fala smiled and looked at Benny. "Sometimes a parent is blind to the fact that her children have grown," she said, and hugged Togo. "I am proud that you stand by the things that you believe, but you shall not stand alone. I will join the fight with you."

"I am pleased that our struggle has gained your support," Benny said. "But are you absolutely sure?"

The Gnomes looked at each other and seemed to be having a conversation only they could hear. After several seconds, Fala turned to Benny. "My son's heart is in this, and I will support him."

"Okay then," Benny said. "Is there a place near the mountains where we can be hidden?"

"Yes," Togo answered. "There is a lake at the base of the large mountain. On the north side of the lake, the trees grow heavy with leaves and the bushes are very thick. We can camp there undetected."

"Good," Benny said. "Connie, are we ready?"

"Yes," she said, and led the twins to where Benny was standing.

"Join hands," Benny instructed.

Jack looked around. "Wait a second," he said. "What about the goat?"

"His service is no longer required," Benny said.

"So we're just going to leave him here?" Jack asked. "Will he be okay?"

"Don't worry," Togo said. "He will find his way back home, I assure you."

Jack looked at the goat, which was grazing beside a small pine tree.

Togo patted Jack on the back. "Please, believe me," Togo said. "He will be fine."

Jack put out his hand and Togo held it, then he grasped his other hand with Fala, and the circle was complete. Benny bowed his head and closed his eyes. A strong wind began to blow around them, encircled them, and then, as quickly as it began, it was gone.

They now stood before a large lake at the base of a mountain. Jack looked up at the mountain. The clean white rocks reflected the sun back into his face, and he had to shield his eyes with his hands. He stepped back, tripped over a rock, and landed in the shallow water at the lake's edge.

"Nice one," Maddie said, laughing along with the others.

Connie came to Jack's side, helped him to his feet, and with a touch on his shoulder, dried his clothes. "Please be more careful," she said.

"I meant to do that," Jack said.

Connie pretended she didn't hear him.

Togo approached Benny. "These bushes should conceal us through the night, and we can meet our mountain cousins in the morning," he informed him.

"We may not have to wait that long," Fala said as a large raven swooped down and landed on Togo's shoulder. The bird crowed softly, and Togo nodded. Then, the raven flew into a nearby tree.

"The chief of the Mountain Gnomes awaits us," Togo said. "We will meet with him and return for you."

"Very well," Benny said. "We have some preparations of our own to make. We will see you soon, and please, be careful."

Fala looked at Benny. "You be careful as well, Benjamin."

Benny nodded and the raven flew out of the tree. Togo waved to Benny and he and Fala followed the large bird.

Twenty-One

"Oww!" Maddie yelled for the third time, as her hair was again caught in the heavy brush between the lake and the mountain, where Benny had them set up camp. Connie helped to free her.

"Do we really need to do this?" Jack asked.

"Yes," Benny said as he waved a hand over his head. "Somehow, Tardon knows we're on the move, and if any of the Tars show up, we need to be hard to find."

"Tars?" Maddie questioned.

"Followers of Tardon," Connie explained as she began to unroll the sleeping bags.

Benny sat on one of the bags and clapped his hands. The bright light appeared again and Jingo emerged from it. "I need your services once again, my friend," Benny said. "Please return to Gavin and tell him to meet me at the north edge of the lake an hour after dark." Jingo nodded and was off, and Benny stretched out on the sleeping bag. "I've cast a charm around us, so we should be safe to rest for a while."

Maddie sat down. "If you cast a charm, how was the fairy able to find us?"

Benny smiled. "I'm glad you're thinking about these things," he said. "Well, first, I summoned Jingo so he knew where we were, and second, different magical beings have different magical powers. What works with one may not work on another. That's something you two should keep in mind."

Jack fell onto one of the sleeping bags and stretched out, with his arms folded behind his head and his legs crossed at the ankles, the way he had on the couch at home so many times before. "I know you want to teach us about the magical world," he said. "But, all I care about is getting Mom and Dad. Do we have a plan for that?"

Maddie rolled her eyes at her brother. "I don't think Jack means to be rude," she said.

Jack sat up. "I didn't think I was being rude," he argued.

"Nor do I," Connie said as she sat down across from Jack. "I understand what you want to accomplish, and it's normal to want to know what course of action we'll take to reach that goal."

"Thank you," Jack said as he looked at his sister. "At least *somebody* understands me."

Benny glanced at Connie and grinned before turning his attention to the twins. "My friend, Gavin, has lived in Tardon's territory for some time, and he has kept a close eye on things. He will be able to tell us if Tardon is keeping your parents here—and where, exactly—and then we can decide on a course of action. I'd like to keep the possibility of us getting killed to a minimum."

"Do you really think we could get killed?" Maddie asked, her voice more than a bit shaky.

Jack stepped close to his sister. "Yes, Maddie," he said. "It is a very real possibility, or haven't you been paying attention? We've been under constant attack since we got here and everything we've learned so far has been to protect ourselves. So, it's possible we will be killed. They know it, I know it, and you better know it."

Maddie exploded into tears and threw herself onto the sleeping bag, burying her face in her arms. Connie shot Jack a disapproving look, and hurried to comfort Maddie.

Benny stood. "Jack!" he scolded. "You come with me."

Jack looked at Benny hard. He could see he had stirred up real anger, but he didn't care. Days ago, Jack never would have thought to say those things out loud. He would never criticize the actions of an adult. He'd been taught to respect his elders, even when he disagreed with them. But things were different now. Jack was in full protection mode. His parents weren't here to keep him and Maddie safe; that job fell on his shoulders now, no matter what role Benny thought he held in their lives.

Jack knew that Benny had dragged them into this mess, and Jack wasn't going to put his trust in him anymore; he wasn't going to put his trust in anyone. The only two people he could count on were now counting on him, and the only help he could rely on was Maddie's. She needed to see things the way he did. They needed to be on the same page, and if it was harsh, then so be it.

Jack stood and followed Benny a short distance from the camp. They stopped walking and Benny turned. He stood close to Jack so that their noses were only inches apart.

"Young man," Benny said. "I know that Connie had a talk with you on the importance of keeping your emotions under control, but you don't seem to have taken to that lesson. Getting yourself worked up and upsetting your sister puts everything in jeopardy."

Jack wasn't backing down. "Everything is already in jeopardy," he said. "Everything we care about, anyway. And how am I supposed to control my emotions? My parents are being held hostage, or they're already dead, and I'm supposed to stay calm."

"Jack," Benny said. "We don't know that."

"Exactly; we don't know anything!" Jack yelled.

"Well, scaring your sister isn't going to help things."

"Are you kidding?" Jack challenged. "She's already scared, and I'm sure she's thinking the same things I am; I just said it out loud, is all." He took several deep breaths to fight back the tears he felt pooling in his eyes.

Benny backed up a few steps. "But you have to stop thinking those things; it doesn't help."

Tears were now running down Jack's face. "I know it doesn't help, but I can't stop thinking it." He took another deep breath. "And I thought you had a plan."

"Believe me, Jack," Benny said. "I have kept you informed of all I know, but I cannot come up with a plan until I've received information from Gavin. When I have, we can piece things together."

"Okay," Jack said. "But when the plan gets made, Maddie and I are going to have a say."

Benny moved close to Jack again and put an arm around his shoulders. "Okay," he said. "As soon as Gavin gets here, we'll talk things out, together."

"Is that him?" Jack asked, looking over Benny's shoulder.

Benny turned and saw two people heading toward him and Jack. "Let's get back to the others," he said. "Gavin's not alone."

They both quickly headed back to the concealment of the bushes. Benny watched, as the two newcomers stopped by the water's edge and took in their surroundings. Then he turned to Connie.

"Gavin's brought Lisa with him. I don't know why, but be ready for anything." Benny eyed the twins and then said, "*All* of you."

Twenty-Two

With darkness falling quickly, it was hard for Benny to see from the bushes what, if anything, the two people approaching were up to. "I'm going to find out what's going on," he said. "Connie, if there's any sign of odd movement, get the twins out of here, fast."

Connie gave Benny a thumbs up, and Benny walked out from the bushes. "Greetings, my friend," he called.

Both of the newcomers turned around. One was tall and thin, and the other short and stocky. They exchanged a few words, and the short one approached Benny.

He was small, but had broad shoulders and thick arms, and seemed a force to be reckoned with. His head was covered with thick, black curly hair, and his beard matched, except for the sprinkling of gray here and there. He extended a hand to Benny and they shook.

"Good to see you, my friend," the man said.

"Gavin, I appreciate you coming and offering your help," Benny said and looked in the direction of the tall thin figure. "But why would you bring her?"

Gavin looked at the ground, sighed, and then focused on Benny again. "I know what you think of Lisa," he said. "But you are wrong."

Benny shook his head. "Are you trying to tell me she's here to help?"

"I can tell you that she's not here to hinder things."

Benny began to pace in front of Gavin. "And how can you be sure?" he asked.

"Lisa's always been neutral," Gavin said.

Benny stopped pacing and walked close to Gavin. He spoke softly. "You know what her husband was; you can't possibly believe that they didn't share similar views."

Gavin put a hand on each of Benny's shoulders. "I can only tell you that the fact that I am here and having this conversation is proof that she means no harm. She's known for some time that I have been giving you information, and she has never uttered a single word about it."

Benny sighed. "Why is she here now?"

"She's concerned for the welfare of the twins," Gavin replied.

Benny's eyes went wide. "She knows they're here? She knows about Ray and Tina?"

Gavin sighed. "My friend, the capture of the parents of the *destined ones* is not something that Tardon has kept secret. He wants all who follow him to know that he can handle any threat to his grand plans."

Benny looked at Gavin for a moment. "And you're convinced that she's concerned for the twins?"

"I am," Gavin said. "After all, she *is* family."

Lisa had grown impatient and walked over to the two men. She announced her arrival. "I don't like standing in the dark alone," she said. "If you gentlemen are done with your hellos, I'd like to meet my niece and nephew."

Lisa was tall and thin, just like her brother Ray. She had long, sandy-colored hair that she had tied back in a long ponytail. Her nose was thin and long, and she lifted it to the sky when she spoke.

"Lisa," Benny said, remembering his manners. "You're looking well."

"Yes, yes," Lisa said as she looked around. "Nice to see you too, Benny, but my family—where are they?"

Benny looked at Gavin and rolled his eyes. "Just one second," Benny said, and took several steps toward Lisa. "These kids have been through a great deal in a short period of time, and they don't even know you exist. I don't want you thinking you can play the doting aunt all of a sudden. You will take a back seat and observe. The twins are under my training and that will continue without any interference. Am I clear?"

Lisa held a hand to her chest. "Of course," she said. "I would never wish to upset them. But please, where are they?"

"One last thing," Benny said. "And this is an absolute. There will be no mention of them being the *destined ones*, the golden children, or any other thing." He paused to look at both Gavin and Lisa, to make certain they understood completely. "This was Ray and Tina's wish from the day the twins were born, and it will remain that way until they decide otherwise."

Lisa looked at Gavin and then at Benny. "I will abide by my brother's wishes without question," she said.

Benny took a step closer to Lisa. "You'd better," he warned.

Connie emerged from the bushes. "Is everything all right?" she called.

"Fine," Benny answered without looking away from Lisa. "Bring Jack and Maddie, and join us."

Connie returned to the bushes, and she came out with the twins following closely behind her. Lisa saw them coming and took a few quick steps toward them. Benny put an arm in front of her to hold her back. She stopped and squinted at Benny. Soon, all the wizards were standing beside the lake in the bright moonlight.

"Connie," Benny said. "You know Gavin, and this is Lisa. She'll be with us for a while." He turned to the twins. "Jack, Maddie," he said. "This is my good friend Gavin; he is a great help to us."

Gavin shook hands with the twins, while Lisa tapped her foot quickly.

Benny looked at her, and then made the introductions. "And this is Lisa."

"*Aunt* Lisa," Lisa said as she stepped toward the twins and gave them each a hug.

Jack and Maddie looked at each other and then at Benny. "Aunt Lisa?" Maddie questioned.

"Yes," Lisa said. "Your father and I are brother and sister, so that makes me your aunt."

Jack and Maddie looked at each other again, then Jack looked at Benny. "This place is just full of surprises," he muttered.

Benny stepped close to the twins and whispered, "I will explain this when I can get you alone."

133

Jack stared at Benny. "I hope you do because..." His sentence was interrupted by the sounds of hooves heading toward them.

"Get behind me!" Benny yelled, and the twins quickly obeyed.

Benny, Connie, and Gavin watched as four, big-horned sheep galloped toward them, each carrying a rider. The wizards took up defensive positions, but by the moonlight Maddie recognized the riders. She came out from the back of the group.

"It's Fala and Togo," she said, and headed toward them.

Lisa went after her and grabbed her arm. "This could be dangerous," she warned. "Let Benny handle it."

Benny stepped forward and looked at Lisa. "She's right," he agreed. "We need to be careful."

Before his sheep came to a complete stop, Togo leapt from it and approached Benny. "We need your immediate help," he said.

The other riders came to a stop and dismounted. Two Gnomes that Benny did not know accompanied Fala. The first was a very old man with a large, white moustache. He was dressed in the same Gnome attire as Togo. The second was a woman, about Togo's age, who was stunningly beautiful, for a Gnome. She wore a simple pink dress, a pink ribbon in her hair, and her eyes were dark and large and held any onlooker spellbound, if just for a second.

Fala made quick introductions. "This is Chief Eton and his daughter, Retta," she said. "Benny, please help."

"Of course I will help you," Benny said. "But with what?"

Togo spoke. "We have received word from the forest animals; our home is under attack as we speak. We must return immediately."

"Are you sure of this?" Benny asked.

"Yes," Fala answered. "We must go and defend our home; only your magic can get us there quickly enough."

"Okay," Benny said. "Everyone stay here. I will go..."

Maddie interrupted. "We're all going."

"Maddie," Jack said. "We need to stay focused on getting Mom and Dad."

Maddie looked hard at him. "Togo and Fala have offered us help; we owe them."

He sighed. "I hate it when you're right."

"That's not a good idea," Benny said.

"Benny, please," Fala said. "There is no time to argue; we must go."

He rolled his eyes. "Fine. We're all going. Everyone join hands."

They all held hands, and in a second, were caught up in a swirling wind.

Twenty-Three

The wind stopped and the group was standing just outside the entrance to the Gnome cave, which was open. There was shouting of directions and screams of pain, echoing through the trees. Jack and Maddie looked around and saw Gnomes running in several directions, and some taking up positions on tops of rocks and in the trees, shooting arrows from their small bows at an adversary that was yet to be revealed.

From the sky came a loud *whoosh,* along with a blast of hot air that knocked the twins and the rest of their group to the ground.

Maddie looked up and grabbed Jack's arm. "Jack!" she yelled.

Jack looked up and saw that the tops of the trees around them were engulfed in flames, and in the sky were four large, green, winged lizards.

"Are those…" he said.

"Dragons," Connie said as she pulled herself and the twins back to their feet. "We need to move."

"My thoughts, exactly," Benny said. "Get the twins to a safe place, and we'll do what we can to help."

Fala grabbed Togo's hand. "Come, we must defend the forest."

They pulled bows and arrows from their backpacks and joined the battle. The two Mountain Gnomes, each brandishing a small sword, followed. Connie grabbed the twins by their hands.

"I'll see to my family," Lisa said as she put an arm around each of the twins.

Benny looked from Connie to Lisa and then at the destruction around him. "Go with them, Connie," he urged, and he headed off with Gavin in the direction of Fala and Togo.

Connie looked around and saw a group of large rocks just in front of them, and there was a small tree behind the rocks.

"Over there," she pointed, and led them to the rocks.

The twins and Lisa hunched down under the tree and behind the group of boulders, which shielded from what was happening around them. A tremendous roar that Jack felt in his chest tore through the forest.

"What the..." Jack said, but before he could say anymore, a giant, hairless, grizzly bear galloped past them in pursuit of two Gnomes.

The bear swiped its frying-pan-sized paw, and its long claws sank into one of the Gnome's back. The Gnome let out a terrible shriek, and blood spurted onto the surrounding plant life.

"No!" Maddie screamed as the bear caught up to the second Gnome, and she covered her eyes as the Gnome screamed in pain.

"I'm going to help," Connie said. "You stay here."

"I will make sure of it," Lisa said.

Connie looked at the twins and Lisa. She didn't know this woman, but she knew that Benny wasn't fond of her. He didn't want Lisa left alone with the twins, but Connie felt the need to help. She looked around. Trees were burning, Gnomes were shooting arrows into the giant bears with little or no effect, and the dragons were hovering overhead. She had to do something.

Another large bear leapt over a fallen tree just in front of Connie, and was about to sink its fangs into a Gnome, when Connie held out a hand and froze the bear. The Gnome turned to Connie, bowed, and returned to the fight.

"Nice one," Benny said, as he joined the group behind the rocks.

"Benny," Connie sighed in relief. "What's going on here?"

"I'm not sure," Benny said. "For some reason the Gici Awas have decided to launch an attack on the Gnomes and have been joined by the dragons. It looks like a full out effort to destroy their home and as many Gnomes as possible."

"Why?" Maddie asked, tears cascading down her face.

"I'm not sure," Benny said. "But if Tardon knew we were coming, he may also have known we were aided by the Gnomes. He most likely sent these creatures to punish the Gnomes for helping us."

"You don't know that, Benny," Lisa argued.

Benny clenched his teeth and looked at Lisa. "Don't start. There's no time now for your opinions."

Jack stood and looked out into the forest. "Isn't that Gavin?" he asked.

Gavin was standing on top of a tree stump, looking toward the sky. "Come on, you flying snakes!" he yelled. "Come and get me!"

The dragons grouped together and seemed to focus on Gavin. The swooped toward him, and Gavin raised both hands over his head. Suddenly, the wings of the dragons were pinned to their sides and they began to spin like an out-of-control helicopter.

One of the dragons crashed into the top of a large pine tree, and tree and dragon collided hard with the ground. Two of the dragons had a mid-air collision and fell out of sight. The fourth made it through the trees and went head first into the ground, sliding several feet before stopping at Gavin's feet. As Gavin looked at the dragon, one of the Gici Awas came running at him from behind. Jack stood, and looked as though he was throwing something. A ball of fire hit the large bear, and it exploded in flames.

Gavin looked in the direction of the fireball and ran to where the other wizards were taking shelter.

"Thanks, kid," Gavin said and patted Jack on the back. Gavin's chest heaved, and he took a deep breath. "There are a lot of those bears around; maybe we should stay here and wait until they tire themselves out."

Maddie stood. "We have to help," she said. "We owe it to Togo and Fala."

Gavin shrugged. "I'm open to ideas."

"We just need to do whatever we can to stop as many as we can," Connie said, and she moved from behind the rocks to send one of the bears flying into a tree. This only seemed to annoy the giant animal. It let out a thunderous roar and leapt for Connie.

Jack jumped on top of the rocks he was hiding behind. "No!" he yelled, and held out a hand in the direction of the Gici Awas.

The bear was taken into the air and held suspended for a moment. Its heart began to beat so loud that everyone heard it, and the beats grew faster and louder. There was a strange ripping sound, and the bear's chest opened and its heart burst sending blood in every direction.

Spurred on by her brother, Maddie also jumped into action. She saw one of the hairless beasts a few yards away, zeroing in on a Gnome that was sending arrow after arrow into it with no effect. Maddie held out a hand and the bear began to shrink—first to the size of a dog, then to that of a rabbit, and finally, to the size of a mouse. It ran off and Maddie looked around.

"There's so many of them," she said. "Why can't they pick on somebody their own size?"

"That's it," Jack said, and took off running.

Benny started to go after him, but he saw Jack stop at the spot where the wizards had appeared only moments before, and pick something up. Jack had Fala's backpack, and he took out the two sticks Fala had used to announce their arrival to the Sasquatch. He banged them together as hard as he could, over and over.

It was only a few moments, but it seemed like forever until a dense clump of bushes was pulled apart just in front of them, and a large, muscular, ape-like man stepped out. He was covered from head to toe in thick black fur, and was twice the size of any man in both height and width. The Sasquatch let out a loud grunt and two of the Gici Awas ran off.

Maddie stood frozen, her mouth opened as wide as her eyes. Jack also looked at the creature in both disbelief and fear, but he swallowed hard and stepped forward.

"The forest Gnomes need your help," he said to the Sasquatch.

The beast looked at Jack and tilted its head to one side as it considered the boy in front of it.

"The Gnomes are being attacked," Jack went on. "Their home is being destroyed and they need help. Now!"

The Sasquatch looked around again and let out a mighty roar. It broke off a large branch from a nearby tree and Jack ducked behind the rocks. The animal began to hit the tree with the branch in series of rhythmic knocks. Within seconds, several more Sasquatch

143

appeared. They were all very large and covered in fur in various shades of brown and red. They grunted among themselves and then, as one of the large hairless bears came into view, they went to the defense of the Gnomes.

One of the Sasquatch grabbed a Gici Awas and threw it into the forest with ease. The others let out loud howls that sent the remaining bears fleeing, and the Sasquatch went in pursuit. Within a few minutes, all was silent in the forest.

Benny put a hand on Jack's shoulder. "Nice job," he commended. "What made you think of summoning the Sasquatch?"

"Well," Jack said. "Maddie said the bears should pick on someone their own size, and I remembered the respect Togo and Fala showed the Sasquatch; I just hoped they had the same respect for the Gnomes."

"You did a fine job," Gavin said. "I'm just wondering how you were able to talk to them."

Connie smiled and put an arm around Jack. "He has a way with animals," she said and kissed Jack on the cheek. "Now, let's find Togo and Fala." She led the way into the forest with Jack, Maddie, and Lisa right behind her.

Gavin tapped Benny on the shoulder. "It looks like he has a way with the young ladies as well," he said. They laughed and went on the search with the others.

There was a great deal of destruction done to the forest. Most of the trees surrounding the entrance to the Gnome cave were burning or lying on the ground. There were puddles of blood all around, and several bodies of Gnomes littered the forest floor. Maddie stopped, and Jack stopped beside her.

"Are you okay?" Jack asked.

Maddie nodded but she had tears in her eyes and her face had gone gray.

"You're not okay," Jack said, and Maddie ran toward a small bush and vomited. "Oh, yeah. That'll make you feel better. Let's keep moving," he told her.

Lisa hurried to Maddie and put an arm around her. She looked at Jack and shook her head. "Do you need to rest?" she asked Maddie.

Maddie shook her head. "No. Jack's right; we need to find Fala and Togo."

Lisa looked ahead at Jack, who was now leading the group. She shook her head again.

Jack stopped just past the cave entrance and the rest of the group did the same. Fala was walking toward them with Chief Eton and his daughter, Retta, on either side of her. They all looked more than a bit battle weary. Their clothes were torn in several places, they'd lost their hats, and there were cuts and bruises on their faces and arms. Behind them, Togo was walking slowly and carrying a large bundle over his shoulder.

Benny, Jack, and Connie ran to them.

"Are you all right?" Benny asked.

"*We* are," Chief Eton answered. "However, not all of us are."

Togo walked in front of the group and placed the bundle on the ground very gently. It was the lifeless body of Chief Rogo.

Twenty-Four

Tears ran down Fala's cheeks as she knelt beside Rogo's body. She kissed him gently on the forehead and held his hand. Togo looked on through tears of his own as, one by one, the forest Gnomes began to gather around the body of their fallen chief. A very old Gnome stepped in front of Togo.

"He must be returned to the forest as soon as possible," the old Gnome said.

Togo nodded and knelt beside his mother. "Mother," he said.

Fala looked at her son and squeezed his hand. "I know," she said, and she kissed Rogo again and rose.

Several Gnomes came forward, carrying very large leaves. They wrapped Rogo's body in the leaves and then picked it up. The body was moved a short distance to a circle of small trees just behind the entrance to the Gnome cave. Rogo's body was placed in the center of the circle, and then the old Gnome stepped forward. He bowed his head.

147

"Our great Mother Nature, we return our Chief, Rogo, to you in the hope that he will help replenish the earth from which he came."

From the ground, the roots of the trees rose around Rogo's body, and within seconds, the roots were wrapped all around him. Then, the roots receded into the ground, taking Rogo's body with them.

Jack looked around. Maddie and Connie were crying silently, Benny and Gavin had their heads bowed, and Lisa had an arm around Maddie. Jack felt sad; Rogo had helped them and he'd paid with his life for giving that help. Still, Jack felt a need to remain on track, a need to find his parents and get home. While Jack wondered how to bring up this subject, the old Gnome approached Togo again.

"We must convene the table," he said.

Togo shook his head. "My mother and I need some time."

Fala wiped away a tear. "No, Togo, he is right. It is custom, and your father would want us to uphold our customs."

Togo smiled. "That is true," he said, and almost laughed. "Father would want that. Very well, convene the table."

The old Gnome nodded, raised his hands to get the attention of all the other Gnomes, and then he led the way into the cave and into the meeting room with the large stone table in the center. The wizards followed, not knowing if they belonged, but also not knowing what else to do.

Benny moved beside Togo. "My friend," Benny whispered. "Should we be here?"

Togo stopped and took Benny's hand. "You have defended our home, and you have saved us from certain doom. Where else should you be?"

Benny bowed his head. "Thank you."

"No," Togo said. "Thank you."

Togo took his place at the table, and the wizards took their seats on the bench off to the side. Jack looked around the cave. A few of the seats at the table were empty, and the crowd was definitely smaller than the last time he was here. Even this meeting room, deep within the Gnome cave, had suffered damage. Part of one of the walls was crumbled, there were several cracks in the ceiling, and the table itself was covered in a layer of dirt and rock dust. Jack's heart sank at the sight of the damage.

The old Gnome stood, and the murmuring in the room stopped. "We first pause to remember our fallen ones," he said and everyone bowed their heads. After several seconds, he continued. "We pay homage to our fallen Chief."

A whispering chant began to go through the room. "Rogo, Rogo, Rogo," the Gnomes said in unison, before the old Gnome raised a hand and all fell silent.

"We must choose our next Chief. Is there a nomination from the table?"

Fala stood. "I nominate Togo," she said.

Togo's eyes went wide, and he leaned close to Fala. "Mother," he whispered. "I am not ready."

Fala took Togo's hand. "My son, you are more than ready."

Another Gnome at the table stood. "I will second the nomination," he said.

Yet another stood. "I offer my endorsement of Togo as well."

The old Gnome raised his hands to the crowd. "Is there need of a vote?" he asked. There was no immediate reply, and the old Gnome pointed at Togo. "I give you: Chief Togo," he said.

A chant, much louder than the one honoring Rogo, went up among the Gnomes. "Togo, Togo, Togo," the Gnomes went on and on, until Togo stood and raised his hands. The room fell silent.

"I accept this great honor," he said. "As your new Chief, I call us to immediate action. Today, we were attacked in an effort to destroy our home. It was only by the actions of our wizard friends that we were saved. Now, we must join their struggle. Tardon corrupts the wildlife. He forces them to do things against their nature, and he has declared war on us. The wizard struggle is now ours as well. Who will join me in this fight?"

Most of the Gnomes rose; it was only the young and very old who did not.

"Thank you," Togo replied. "I will ask the Sasquatch to stand guard over those that remain, and the rest of us will take this fight to Tardon."

Togo and Fala walked from the table to where the wizards were sitting. Togo leaned close to Benny. "Am I assuming too much by thinking we will resume the quest to find the young ones' parents?"

Jack, who sat next to Benny, answered. "No, you assume correctly. We leave in the morning."

Jack then walked out of the meeting room, and the other wizards followed as Togo received congratulations from the Gnomes. Jack went back to the small cave where they had stayed the night before the start of their journey. It looked the same, but things had definitely changed.

Jack sat by the small fire in the center of the cave. Connie sat on his right and Maddie on his left. Lisa stayed close to Maddie. Benny and Gavin sat across from the twins on the other side of the fire.

"Listen," Benny said. "Before we begin to lead the Gnomes…"

Jack cut across him. "Gavin," he said. "I've been told that you live in Tardon's territory. Do you have any idea where he may be keeping my parents?"

Benny looked hard at Jack, and Gavin looked at Benny. There was silence for several seconds until Jack snapped his fingers. "Are you with us Gavin?" he asked.

Gavin continued to look at Benny. When Benny shrugged, Gavin answered. "Tardon has a small village near the top of the highest mountain. He has centered his followers there recently, and it is believed this is because he is keeping Ray and Tina there."

"Okay," Jack said. "We're going to have to plan this carefully; a straightforward attack is out of the question. Even with the Gnomes, I assume we'll be outnumbered."

"Well," Lisa said. "I'm glad you're thinking, because an attack on Tardon is not a wise thing, especially since you don't even know that he was responsible for what happened here..."

Jack was now on a roll and Lisa was in his path. "Lady, I don't even know who you are, and I'm certainly not interested in your opinions. But, just so you know where I'm coming from, I don't care if Tardon ordered this attack on the Gnomes. He took my parents, and I'm going to get them back." He looked at Maddie. "We're going to get them back." He then put a hand out toward Maddie, but Lisa put an arm around her.

"She's very upset," Lisa said. "She could do with a little comforting, and you don't seem to be equipped for that."

Jack ignored Lisa and took Maddie by the hand. "Maddie, come with me." He pointed at Benny. "You too."

Jack led the way to a corner of the cave. "Benny," he said. "You promised us answers, so let's start with who this lady is."

Benny ignored Jack's change in demeanor. "Lisa is your father's sister, and a very good wizard."

"But you don't like her," Maddie said.

"I don't *trust* her," Benny answered. "I'm not sure what she stands for. She's always professed to be neutral in this battle, but her husband gave his loyalty to Tardon."

"So he fought against you?" Maddie asked.

"Not in a straight-up fight, but he recruited heavily for Tardon and spread his message to anyone who would listen. Lisa never helped him, but she never spoke out against him either, and after her husband's death, she claimed to be neutral..."

"You don't believe her," Jack said.

"Knowing who her husband was, and the fact that they shared a home and a life, it makes me wonder, but Gavin believes her, and that does carry some weight with me."

"Okay," Jack said. "So we'll keep an eye on her. Maddie, don't get too close to her."

"But she's been nice to me," Maddie protested.

"I know that," Jack said. "But we don't know her, so please, don't get too close."

"Okay," Maddie said, and she returned to her spot by the fire.

"Thanks, Benny," Jack said. "Now let's get some rest. I want to be at the mountain first thing in the morning."

Benny watched Jack walk back to the fire. He liked that Jack was focused in his desire to rescue Ray and Tina, but there seemed to be something reckless in it too. He'd have to keep a close watch.

Jack sat close to Connie when he returned to the fire. He leaned close and whispered, "I need a favor."

"If I can," Connie said.

"Benny doesn't trust this woman Lisa, and I don't know her. Would you keep an eye on her, and make sure she doesn't try to stop our mission?"

Connie looked over at Lisa, who was again sitting beside Maddie. "I can do that," she said.

"Thanks," Jack said. "I knew you were someone I could count on." Jack spread out beside the fire with his hands folded behind his head and his feet crossed at the ankles.

Twenty-Five

As everyone slept, Jack moved quietly to where Maddie was lying. He shook her gently several times before she opened her eyes. She squinted and stretched as she struggled to wake. "Jack," she said. "Is everything okay?"

Jack whispered. "I just want to talk to you. Come over here." He indicated the spot in the corner where he'd spoken to her earlier.

They sat on the cold ground and Maddie stretched. "What is it?" she asked.

"I want you to keep your distance from Lisa," Jack said.

"This again," Maddie said. "Jack, she's been very nice to me."

Jack smirked. "I've seen that she looks like she cares about you, but…"

"But what?" Maddie interrupted. "You don't think I can take care of myself. I've heard what Benny's said about her, but I can make up my own mind about people."

Jack sighed. "I know that, but it's just that ever since we got here, nothing makes any sense and we don't even know her."

Maddie shook her head. "She's our aunt, Jack, and in case you haven't noticed, we're a little short on family right now."

Jack took a deep breath. He thought about what Connie had said about keeping his emotions under control, and he really didn't want to get angry with Maddie.

"Okay," Jack said. "So she's our aunt; that doesn't mean she's a good person or on our side."

Maddie pleaded with her brother. "Oh, come on, Jack; you have to trust somebody at some point."

Jack took Maddie's hand. "You're the only one I trust," he said. "I don't believe anything anyone here says, and I want to stay focused on getting Mom and Dad and getting home. I need you to stay focused with me."

"And stay away from Lisa," Maddie repeated.

"I just want you to be careful."

"Remember what I said, Jack," Maddie reminded him as she got up. "I can take care of myself."

Maddie returned to her spot by the fire, and Jack thought about going back to his own place in the warmth, but didn't move. The distance between him and the others felt comfortable, and he leaned against the cave wall to stare at the fire.

Morning came quickly, and Jack saw that someone had left a basket of bread and fruit by the entrance, so he must have fallen asleep at some point. He stood and stretched. It was time to get moving.

"Okay, everyone!" Jack shouted, stirring the group. "Let's get this show started."

Benny was already on his feet and walked over to Jack. "I think we need to make a plan before we do anything," he said.

Jack looked at Benny. He'd loved Benny not too long ago, and somewhere inside he still did, but he was done taking orders. "I will," Jack said. "After I see what we're up against. Right now, I just want to get to that mountain, and we'll take it from there."

Benny put a hand on Jack's shoulder. "I'm not sure that's wise," he warned.

Jack pulled away. "Then you don't have to come," he said and walked away.

After eating quickly, Jack addressed the group again. "Let's get everything we need and let's get moving." No one questioned him, and in minutes, Jack led them out of the cave and into the forest.

As they stepped into the forest, the wizards saw that Togo and Fala, and a large group of Gnomes were was waiting. Togo greeted them and then addressed Benny.

"We are prepared for anything and are at your command," he said.

Benny patted Togo's shoulder. "I appreciate that, my friend. But it appears that young Jack has taken control."

Togo looked at Jack and then back at Benny. He scratched his head. "Do you believe that's wise?" he asked.

Gavin had moved beside Benny. "I was thinking the same thing," he said. "We can't take a backseat to this kid. He doesn't know Tardon's power, or even much of anything."

Benny held up a hand to calm Gavin. "Let's see what happens for now. I know Jack better than he believes, and I have faith in his ability. But, to ease your concerns, I will stay close by."

"I believe in you, Benny," Gavin said. "And I trust your judgment; I just hope you know what you're doing this time."

Gavin and Togo left Benny, and Benny took another look at Jack. "So do I," he said to himself.

As they readied to leave, Maddie absorbed the destruction of the forest. Her eyes filled with tears and her stomach turned. For a second, she thought she might have been sick again, but she took a deep breath and steadied herself. She looked at Lisa who was standing beside her.

"This is terrible," Maddie said. "Why would anyone do this?"

Lisa put an arm around Maddie, as was quickly becoming her habit. "I have a theory," she said.

The sadness on Maddie's face prompted Lisa to explain.

"I know that Benny is quick to blame Tardon," Lisa said. "And that would be the conventional thinking among a great many wizards, but you have to look at the facts. For centuries, the Gnomes have lived in this forest and looked after the balance of things; they've never taken into account that they could be disturbing the balance they seek to protect."

Maddie took a step back. "How would they do that?" she asked.

"The Gnomes choose which animals to protect," Lisa said. "They decide which ones get to live in the forest, and they've driven out many creatures that they believe disturb the balance—the Gici Awas among them. Perhaps these creatures simply decided to take back what rightfully belongs to them."

Maddie looked at Lisa with wide eyes. "Do you really think that's what happened?"

"I can't be sure," Lisa said. "It's just a possibility. You should learn now: not everything is the way it seems."

Jack called out, "Maddie, come over here by me."

Maddie began to walk toward Jack.

"He orders you around quite a bit," Lisa observed.

Maddie shrugged and went over to join her brother.

"Stay close to me," Jack said. Maddie nodded, and Jack turned to Connie. "I need you close by, too."

Connie looked to where Benny was standing with the Gnomes and Gavin. Lisa joined that group. "Okay, Jack," Connie said.

"Benny," Jack said. "I think we're ready; take us to the highest mountain."

Benny and Gavin exchanged looks and then Benny raised his hands.

162

Twenty-Six

A moment later, they were standing among rocks and gravel at the base of a large mountain. With the sun reflecting off the rocks, it was easy to see why these were called the White Mountains. They had to shield their eyes just to look in the direction of the largest mountain. Chief Eton went into his backpack and handed out sunglasses to everyone. Jack chuckled to himself. Magic, it seemed, couldn't remedy every situation.

"Gavin," Jack said, and Gavin stepped forward. "Do you think we could appear outside Tardon's hideout, or is this one of those times when magic wouldn't be useful?"

Gavin took a moment. He didn't know Jack at all, but he didn't like this kid very much. "Sure," he said. "We could just pop in on Tardon. I'm sure he'll be glad to see us, maybe offer us some refreshments, and if we ask real nice, he'll just hand over Ray and Tina."

Jack took two steps toward Gavin so that he was almost too close. "Listen," he said. "I'm not in the mood for any attitude. I'm just trying to figure out the best way to go about this; I don't need you to make fun of me."

Benny stepped between them. "Jack, I don't think Gavin's trying to belittle you in any way. I think he's just trying to point out that a more experienced hand maybe better suited to handle this situation."

"Fine," Jack said. "I'll ask someone more experienced. Connie, what do you think?"

Connie looked at Benny, and he shrugged and gave her a small smile that said he was okay with this, for now.

"Well," Connie said. "It looks like it would be a long and difficult hike to the top of the mountain, but if there is a place we could appear undetected, then magic might be our best option."

Retta, Chief Eton's daughter, stepped forward. "There is a way we can reach the top without anyone seeing us," she said.

Chief Eton took his daughter by the arm and turned her toward him. Retta," he said. "I know what you're thinking, but that is a secret and sacred pathway to be used only in time of most dire emergencies."

"Forgive me, Father," Retta said. "But Tardon is holding their parents, and who knows what he may do. This is a time of dire emergency, and we must aid those who have helped our kind."

Chief Eton hung his head. "Forgive me, Great Mother, for my selfishness," he said and then looked at Retta again. "You have learned well."

Jack cleared his throat. "If you can help us, now would be a great time to let us in on the secret."

Retta explained. "Over the centuries, in order to protect ourselves, we have built pathways under the mountains. They lead everywhere. However, we have sworn an oath to our Great Mother Nature that they were to be used only in times of great need. Otherwise, she would never have blessed our digging of her ground."

"Does this qualify as great need?" Maddie asked.

"We shall see," Chief Eton said. "Come."

He moved to the head of the group and led them up a small gravel path only a few hundred yards long. At the end, the way forward was blocked by two large rocks. Chief Eton and Retta knelt before the rocks. Chief Eton then turned to Togo.

"Chief Togo," he said. "Perhaps you and your mother could assist us."

Togo looked at Fala, and she was smiling at having heard her son addressed as Chief. She felt sadness at the loss of Rogo, but she knew he had returned to the earth, and that one day, she would share a place there with him.

Now, she felt pride in her son having ascended to his place.

"Let's see if we can help," she said.

Togo and Fala knelt beside the Mountain Gnomes, and the other Gnomes knelt where they were.

"We must ask for a blessing so the pathway will be opened," Chief Eton explained. He raised his arms. "Our Great Mother," he said. "The young ones traveling with us are in need of help. We ask that you open the passage so that we made aid them in safety."

He bowed his head and all the Gnomes did the same, but nothing happened. After a few minutes, Chief Eton stood. He turned to Jack. "I'm sorry," he said.

"Thank you for trying," Jack said. "Could you tell us if there is a concealed section of the mountain where we could appear?"

"I don't believe it would be wise to use magic so close to Tardon," Benny said. "I'm sure he'll have defenses in place to detect any intruders."

"Benny's right," Connie said. "We'll just have to hike it."

"Lisa," Jack said, ignoring Connie and Benny. "What do you know about Tardon's defenses?"

Benny looked at Jack. No one had openly accused Lisa of following Tardon, and now Jack was asking about her knowledge of Tardon's thinking.

"What makes you think I know anything?" Lisa asked, her nose nearly straight up in the air.

"Jack's only asking," Maddie said, trying to cover her brother's lack of tact.

"I don't like what he's asking, or why," Lisa said.

"Maybe we should just start hiking," Gavin chimed in.

Maddie looked at the rocks. "Just a second," she said, and walked in front of the rocks. She put one hand on each of them and bowed her head. "Great Mother Nature," she said. "My mother and father may be in danger, they may be hurt, and we need to help them. May we use the passage to get to them safely?"

There was a great shaking of the ground, and everyone nearly fell over as the two large rocks separated to reveal the rest of the path.

Jack walked over to Maddie and patted her on the back. "You're amazing, Sis," he said. "Chief Eton, would you like to lead the way?"

The Gnomes were whispering among themselves as Chief Eton moved forward and began to lead the group down the path.

As they began to move forward, Togo paused in front of Benny. "Surely, these are the *destined ones*," he said and continued to move with the others.

Gavin walked beside Benny. "I hope you can keep the *destined ones* in check before they get us all killed."

"I can always count on you for a word of encouragement," Benny retorted, and they began to move with the rest of the group.

Twenty-Seven

The path led into the mountain and gradually sloped upward, but it was not difficult to walk. Being inside the mountain, the group no longer had need of the sunglasses and returned them to Chief Eton. With rock walls on both sides of him and a gravel pathway, Jack felt as though he was being led to an ancient dungeon. He hoped the trust he placed in the Gnomes wouldn't come back to haunt him.

As they walked, Benny caught up to Connie and grabbed the back of her shirt to slow her down. "Stay by me," he said. "We need to talk."

Connie slowed up so that she and Benny were alone at the back of the group.

"I need to know what Jack has planned" Benny said, as he looked around and lowered his voice. "I need you to read his feelings."

Connie stopped. "You know how I feel about that; that's a violation of someone's privacy. It's something I'd only use as a last resort."

"Connie," Benny pleaded. "Jack's leading us into very dangerous territory and we need to be prepared. Please, I need to know what's going on, for his own good and ours."

Connie got the point. She closed her eyes. A mist came from her and headed to Jack. It seemed to go inside of him but he felt and noticed nothing; he just kept walking. After several seconds, the mist left Jack and returned to Connie. She opened her eyes suddenly, as if rudely awakened and slumped against the rock wall.

Benny held her shoulders and steadied her. "Are you all right?" he asked.

Connie took several deep breaths. "He's very strong," she said and looked ahead at the group moving away. "We need to keep up," she said and they started walking again.

"What's going on with him?" Benny asked.

"He has a great deal of conflict inside of him," Connie said. "He's worried about Maddie, he's worried about his parents, and he's very afraid."

"I'd be concerned if he wasn't," Benny said. "Facing Tardon won't be easy."

"He's not afraid of Tardon," Connie said. "He's afraid of you."

Benny stopped. "He's afraid of me?!" he asked in disbelief. "I've taken care of that boy his whole life; I'm the last person he needs to be afraid of."

"That's not how he sees it," Connie said, urging Benny to keep walking. "He believes that you haven't been truthful with him. He resents that you've brought him here from life he was very comfortable with, and he blames you for his parents being taken by Tardon. He doesn't believe that you have his and Maddie's best interests at heart. He believes there's more going on and doesn't understand why you haven't told him everything."

Benny scratched his head. "There are things he's just not ready to hear right now," he said.

"Like the truth about his fate?" Connie questioned.

"Connie," Benny said. "Don't you think I *want* to tell him? It's just that with the circumstances being what they are, I can't have Jack believing he can take on Tardon alone. You've seen how emotional Jack can be. Do you think he's ready to know the truth?"

Connie shrugged. "They have to find out sooner or later."

"They will," Benny said. "But I think it's best that Ray and Tina explain things to them."

"What if they never get the chance?" Connie asked.

"Let's not think that way," Benny said. "I'd like to keep to Ray and Tina's wishes, and let them tell the twins the truth."

Connie shrugged. "Well, since you're usually right, I'll trust you."

Benny smiled. "Thank you. I wish I could get that kind of trust from Jack."

While the group moved on in near silence, Lisa kept her now familiar place beside Maddie.

"You know," Lisa said. "I've been watching your brother, and I have to say that he doesn't seem very nice."

Maddie looked at Lisa. "Why would you say something like that? You don't even know him."

"Well," Lisa said. "From what I've seen, he has a lot of people who are trying to help him and all he's done is been bossy with them. He's completely pushed Benny aside, and Benny can help him more than anyone."

Maddie defended her brother. "Jack just wants to get Mom and Dad back, that's all."

"Alienating the people he needs isn't going to accomplish that," Lisa said. "And the way he treats you is appalling."

Maddie stopped. "Stop it!" she screamed. "Jack loves me, and he just wants me to be safe."

Lisa held her nose in the air. "Really?" she asked. "It seems to me that he takes every opportunity to control you."

Maddie took offense at this statement. "You can't make a statement like that," she said. "You've only just met us; you don't know us at all."

Lisa sighed. "Well, what I've seen is that he tells you where to stand, who to talk to, and even where you should sleep. I think you should start sticking up for yourself at some point, or you'll be in his shadow forever."

Maddie backed away from Lisa. "Jack and I are equals. He needs me, and he knows it. He confides everything in me."

"Does he now?" Lisa questioned, her nose even higher in the air than usual. "So, then, you know what he has planned to get your mother and father?"

Maddie looked at the ground. "Well, no, but…"

"But nothing," Lisa interrupted. "Ray and Tina are your parents too, and if Jack's going to do something to put you and them in danger, you should have a say—before things go terribly wrong."

"Jack wouldn't do anything to hurt me," Maddie argued.

"Maybe not intentionally," Lisa said. "But by acting without consulting anyone, he just might." Lisa held Maddie's hand. "I'm just saying that you need to be more assertive, and to protect yourself."

She squeezed Maddie's hand, let go, and walked away. Maddie watched Lisa move away, scratched her head, and then moved to catch up with everyone else.

Twenty-Eight

The group walked on for hours with Chief Eton and Retta leading the way. Jack was close behind them. He hadn't spoken to anyone the whole time; he simply walked with his eyes fixed straight ahead. His thoughts were nearly nonexistent, his breathing was measured, but his heart rate was slightly accelerated. He didn't know what was going to happen when they finally met Tardon, but the unknown seemed to push him forward.

They reached a point in the path where it forked. Chief Eton stopped and waited for the group to catch up.

"My daughter will lead you from here," he said. "I will return to my people to bring re-enforcements, and I will meet you at the peak." He then turned to address Togo. "I think you should come with me to explain what has happened to your home, so that my people will understand what we must do and why."

Togo bowed to the Chief, and turned to Fala. "Mother, you will lead in my absence."

"Be safe, my son," Fala said, and Togo and Chief Eton took the fork to the right.

Retta stepped forward. "We still have quite a way to travel. Perhaps we should rest."

Jack looked at the fairly large group, focusing on Maddie. Lisa was still right beside her, and Jack didn't like that. "Okay," he said. "We can take a short break."

While most of the group sat and relaxed, Jack joined the other wizards. Benny, Connie, and Gavin were sitting on one side of the path, reclining against the rock wall. Lisa and Maddie sat on the opposite side of the path, both leaning back with their eyes closed.

Jack addressed Gavin. "We need to talk."

Benny stood. "I've been waiting for this," he said.

Jack glared at Benny. "Not you," he said, and motioned to Gavin. "*Him.*"

Benny looked at Gavin and then back at Jack. "Okay," he said, and sat down again.

Gavin got up. "Okay, kid," he said, and followed Jack down the path away from the others. They sat among a group of small boulders and Jack stared at the ground for a bit, drawing lines in the damp gravel with his foot.

"So," Gavin said. "What do you want from me?"

Jack looked at him but didn't speak. He stared at the hard lines in Gavin's face, wondering if this was someone he could trust to tell him the truth. Then he took a deep breath. "Benny tells me that you're friends with Lisa."

Gavin smiled. "I'm not sure that Lisa has any friends, but we talk from time to time, so I guess friend is as good a word as any."

"Can she be trusted?" Jack asked.

"You've spoken to Benny about her," Gavin said.

"Yes," Jack affirmed. "But I want to know from you: can she be trusted?"

Gavin looked Jack straight in the eyes. "It's true that Lisa's husband was a follower of Tardon's. He bought what Tardon sells in big bags, but Lisa never did."

"How can you be sure?" Jack asked.

"We can never be one hundred percent sure about anyone," Gavin answered. "But Lisa's never taken sides. She's stayed neutral, and that couldn't have been easy being married to Baxter."

"What happened to her husband?"

"He was killed in a battle with Stanton's guard."

"And that didn't make her angry enough to side with Tardon?" Jack asked.

"Look," Gavin said. "All I can tell you is that Lisa has known my leaning for a long time. She knows I've been working with Benny and Stanton, and she could have easily turned me over to the Tars, but she never has. For me, that counts as something."

"Okay," Jack said. "But why is she hanging onto my sister like a leech?"

"She's her aunt," Gavin said.

"She's my aunt, too," Jack argued. "But you don't see me getting all cuddly with her."

Gavin laughed. "You're not exactly the cuddly type, kid."

Jack laughed too. "Okay, you can have that one," he said. "But seriously, what's she trying to do with Maddie?"

"Get to know her, I think," Gavin said. "Lisa has no children, and you and Maddie are her family. I think she wants to take care of you both because your mom and dad aren't here right now. She's latched onto Maddie because you haven't even given her a chance."

Jack looked hard at Gavin again. He was in no mood for a lecture on showing respect to his elders. He stood. "Thanks," he said.

"Wait a second," Gavin said. "I have a question for you."

Jack had no idea why, but he sat back down. "Shoot."

"Well," Gavin began. "Since you seem intent on leading us into something you know nothing about, I was wondering if you had a plan, and if you thought about consulting some of us with a bit more experience in these matters?"

Jack shrugged. "No, and no," he said in a very matter-of-fact way.

Gavin rubbed his chin. "That's reassuring," he said.

"When we get to where Tardon's keeping my parents, I'll figure something out," Jack said.

"And you're going to work out this plan all by yourself," Gavin said.

Jack stood. "When we see what's going on and what we're really up against, I'll consult everyone. Okay?"

Gavin stood as well. "Okay, Jack," he said. "I'll take you as a man of your word for now."

Jack watched Gavin walk back to his seat with Benny and Connie. Gavin had called him a man and it felt good.

Gavin sat between Connie and Benny. "So," Benny said, addressing Gavin. "What was that all about?"

"He's worried about Lisa getting too close to his sister," Gavin said. "He wanted to know what I knew about her."

Benny stared at him. "And you gave him the 'Lisa's all warm and fuzzy' story, didn't you?"

Gavin bit his lip. "No," he said. "I told him the truth about my experience with Lisa. I think he's smart enough to make up his own mind."

"Okay," Benny said, choosing not to get into an argument with Gavin. "What do you think about Jack?"

"I think he's way too cocky for his own good," Gavin replied.

Benny smiled. "Yeah. Kind of reminds me of someone."

Twenty-Nine

After their short break, the group walked on for most of the rest of the day. The path had become more and more gradually inclined, and the last few hundred yards seemed to go straight up, but Jack barely felt it. He was being driven by the desire to free his parents and get back to his normal teenage life.

Fala and Retta lead the group and stopped before a large boulder blocking the path. Retta turned to Jack, who was right behind her.

"This is the end of the path," she said. "The peak of the highest mountain is just on the other side of the boulder."

"How do we move it?" Jack asked.

"I will take care of it," Retta said, and she put her hands on the boulder. "Great Mother, thank you for your blessing and for use of your mountain. Our journey is complete."

Gradually, the boulder began to fade, and when it was gone, there was an opening to the outside. Benny walked to the head of the group.

"We need to be ready for anything," Benny said. "There may be guards right outside or magical defenses blocking our way; anything is possible."

"Then maybe a couple of us should check it out," Jack suggested.

"That's a good idea," Benny agreed. "Connie, Gavin, come with me."

"Not exactly what I was thinking," Jack said. "Connie, Maddie, come on. We'll go take a look around."

Benny was speechless as he watched the three youngsters slowly walk through the opening and out to the mountain. Gavin stepped beside Benny. "I don't care if that kid likes it or not; I'm following them," he said.

"Good man," Benny said, as Gavin walked through the opening a few steps behind Maddie.

The hidden path opened onto a small clearing surrounded by rocks. The wind was strong and it was much colder here than at the base. Jack climbed on top of one of the rocks and looked down. In the dusk that was beginning to fall, he could see that just below was a small village, encircled by a rock wall. There were three buildings that looked like large log cabins. He heard a shuffling and turned quickly, but it was only Maddie and Connie peeking over to see what he saw.

"So," Maddie questioned. "This is where Mom and Dad are?"

Jack didn't look at her. "I hope so," he replied. "We just have to figure out a way in, and where Mom and Dad are being kept."

"Yeah, and I'm sure that'll be easy," Gavin said as he walked up behind them.

The shock of the unexpected voice made Jack slip and he fell back onto the clearing. "What are you doing here?" he gasped as he picked himself up.

"I just wanted to make sure you didn't do anything stupid," Gavin said. "And it sounds like I got here just in time."

Jack disregarded Gavin's remark, and watched Maddie and Connie come down from the rock.

"What do you think, Gavin?" Connie asked.

"Well we can't just march in there," he said. "I assume you've noticed the guard."

Jack hadn't and peeked over the rock again. This time he saw that there were two towers at the corners of the wall surrounding the village, and at each tower was a large dragon. Jack climbed down.

"Those dragons will spot you before you even get close, and they'll waste little time roasting you for a quick snack," Gavin said.

"Okay," Jack said. "Do you have a suggestion?"

Gavin winked at Jack, acknowledging that Jack had kept his word and asked for help when he needed it.

"It's probably best if we wait until dark," Gavin advised. "Then we can send a patrol group out to get a feel of the place, and maybe get an idea where Ray and Tina might be held."

"I'm getting tired of waiting," Jack protested. "We need to do *something*."

"Jack," Connie scolded. "Remember our talk about emotions?"

"I remember," Jack whispered.

"Waiting until dark is a good idea," Maddie said. "Maybe the dragons will fall asleep and we can get inside."

Jack didn't like waiting, but he had to admit, if only to himself, that it was a good idea. "Okay," he said. "Let's go back to the others and wait until dark." He then looked at Connie. "Maybe we can come up with something by then."

They returned to the hidden path and found that Chief Eton and Togo had returned with several Mountain Gnomes that were getting acquainted with their forest cousins. Benny was sitting by himself, and Gavin went over and sat beside him.

"So?" Benny asked.

"Tardon has a small village, only three buildings," Gavin explained. "It's encircled with a rock wall, and he has two dragons posted as guards."

"Any wizards?" Benny inquired.

"I didn't see any, but I'd guess there's plenty."

"And magical defenses," Benny added.

"Probably," Gavin said. "I've been able to buy us a couple of hours by suggesting we wait until dark to do anything. I'm hoping you can take control of this expedition by then."

Benny sighed and Gavin stared at him for a moment.

"You have no intention of doing that," Gavin stated.

"No," Benny said. "But I will make certain that Ray and Tina are returned to us and that we stay safe, but I will allow the twins to test their strength."

Gavin cleared his throat. "You realize that could have disastrous results."

185

Cris Pasqueralle

Benny stood. "I don't think it will," he said and walked away.

Benny found Jack sitting just inside the opening of the passage, staring out at the quickly falling darkness, and sat beside him.

"Do you have a plan?" Benny asked.

Jack looked at Benny. "I have an idea," he said.

"And are you going to share what that would be?"

"Yes," Jack said. "With those who have a need to know."

"You know," Benny said. "You asked me to keep you informed of things; I'd like the same courtesy."

"Don't act like you've done that," Jack said. "When you decide to really keep me informed, I'll do the same." He stood. "Now, I need to speak to my sister."

Jack headed to where Maddie was sitting with Lisa, but this time Connie was with them.

"Excuse me, Lisa," Jack said. "I need to talk to Maddie and Connie." He looked around. "Alone, please."

Lisa looked at Maddie and then at Jack. "At least you said please," she said, and got up slowly and walked away.

186

Jack sat between the two girls. "Maddie," he said. "That self-projecting thing: can you do it whenever you want?"

Maddie shrugged. "I guess so. Why?"

Jack ignored the question and addressed Connie. "When she does this thing, the image is faint, like a ghost, right?"

Connie smiled. She understood where Jack was heading. "Yes," she said. "It's very difficult to see."

"So in the dark, she'd be almost invisible?"

"Just about," Connie confirmed.

"Excuse me," Maddie interjected. "Would somebody tell me what we're talking about?"

"You can get into the village," Jack began. "And..."

Maddie caught on and smiled as she finished Jack's sentence. "Find out where they're keeping Mom and Dad."

"Exactly," Jack said.

Maddie hugged her brother. "You're a genius!" she exclaimed.

"That is a great idea," Connie added.

"Well, I'm not just a pretty face," Jack said, and he looked over at Benny who was still sitting where Jack had left him minutes ago, but he had been joined by

Gavin and Lisa. Jack stood. "I'd better go fill in the troops," he said, and walked back toward Benny, followed by Connie and Maddie.

"Jack has an idea how to find out where Mom and Dad are being kept," Maddie announced.

"Oh, yeah?" Gavin asked. "I hope it doesn't involve getting us killed."

Benny looked at Gavin. "Let's hear what he has to say," Benny said. "Go ahead, Jack."

"Well," Jack said. "I was thinking that the image Maddie puts out when she self-projects would be hard to see in the dark, and maybe she could use that to sneak around to see if Mom and Dad are in one of those buildings. Once we know where they are, we could then figure out a way to get to them."

Gavin leaned back against the rock wall and rubbed his chin. "That's not bad, kid," he said.

"I thought it was very smart," Connie said, drawing a smile from Benny.

Jack went on. "While Maddie's doing her thing, I thought the rest of us should act as lookouts, just in case."

Benny rubbed his chin. "That's very good, Jack," he commended. "And as soon as it's dark enough, we'll get started."

"It might be dark enough now," Connie suggested.

Benny looked out the opening. "It does seem pretty dark; let's give it a shot."

They all got up, and Benny went to explain to the Gnomes what was happening, while Jack turned his attention to Lisa.

"I think you should wait here," he said.

Lisa looked at Jack and then at Maddie.

"Jack!" Maddie said.

"Maddie," Jack said. "I'd feel more comfortable if she'd stay here."

Maddie looked at her brother, sighed, and then turned to Lisa. "Maybe you should just wait here," she said.

Lisa didn't put up a fight; she simply sat down with her back to the group.

"That wasn't very nice, Jack," Maddie scolded.

Jack shrugged. "I'm not here to make friends. Now, let's get moving."

They carefully walked out of the opening and onto the clearing. It was dark, with only dim light coming from the cloud obstructed moon. Jack climbed the boulders and looked down on the village. Like before, there was no one around, except for the dragons still keeping watch. He came down.

"There's no one around except for the dragons," he said. "I hope they won't be able to see Maddie's image in the dark."

"We all do," Benny agreed. "I think we should get closer to make this easier for Maddie."

They made their way through a narrow gap between the boulders and slowly climbed down over rocks toward the village. They reached a ledge where they could see the entire village, but were close enough to hear any disturbances, or a cry for help.

Benny turned to Maddie. "Are you ready?" he asked.

Maddie nodded, and Jack put an arm around her. "Okay, Sis," he said. "We have your back."

Maddie took a deep breath and then sat against a large rock. She stared down at the village for several seconds and then closed her eyes.

A nearly transparent version of Maddie stepped out of the actual Maddie, looked at the group, and then walked down to the village. The others watched, barely able to make out the image of Maddie as it climbed over the rock wall and entered Tardon's village. One of the dragons lifted its head and sniffed at the air. Detecting nothing, it lowered its head again. Maddie's image began to walk from building to building, finding a way to look inside at each one. At the smallest building, there was a small window on the side, and after the image had looked inside, it looked up at the group.

"She found them," Jack said.

"And something found her," Gavin said.

Jack looked down at the village and saw that one of the dragons had left its perch and was walking around the grounds. It seemed to know that someone was there but it couldn't see anyone.

"I think it's too dark for them to see her," Benny said. "If she moves slowly, she should be okay."

"What do you mean she 'should be okay?'" Jack asked. "They can't hurt the image, can they?"

"No," Connie said. "But they could scare her enough to cause something to happen to the real Maddie."

"We have to get her out of there," Jack urged.

"We have to break her concentration," Gavin explained. "The image will vanish once she stops thinking about it."

"Then do it," Jack commanded, his whole body beginning to tremble.

"You know her best, Jack," Benny said. "You have to do it."

Jack knelt beside the real Maddie.

"You have to be calm, Jack," Connie instructed. "You can't alarm her."

Jack nodded "Okay, what do I do?"

"Just call her name gently, like you were trying to wake her up," Connie said. "That should be enough to break her concentration."

Jack touched Maddie's shoulder and whispered. "Maddie," he said. "That's enough; you can come back now. Come on, Maddie."

Jack looked down at the village and saw the dragon moving beside the small building, only a few feet from Maddie's image.

"Maddie," he said, a bit louder. "Come back, now."

Maddie's eyes opened and the image Maddie in the village vanished. The dragon sniffed around a bit more and then flew back to its perch.

Jack sighed. "Are you okay, Maddie?' he asked.

"Fine," she said. It seemed that she hadn't noticed the dragon at all. "Mom and Dad are in the small building."

"There must be some kind of protection around that building," Gavin guessed.

"I don't think so," Maddie said. "I mean, wouldn't some kind of magical protection have detected even an image of myself?"

"Not necessarily," Benny said. "But you do make a good point, and it would fit that Tardon would be arrogant enough to assume no one could find his village."

"Let's get in and out as fast as we can, and we can be done with this," Jack said.

"Hold on, kid," Gavin said. "I'm not going to assume there's no protection just because it didn't pick up Maddie's image. We need to be ready."

"No, we need to go now," Jack argued. "Our combined magic should be enough to bypass any protections."

"It might be," Benny agreed. "But I'd still like to get in undetected."

"What if we asked the Gnomes to cause a distraction?" Maddie asked.

"Yeah," Connie agreed. "The Mountain Gnomes live here; they could come across the village by *accident*."

"We'd be asking an awful lot from them," Benny said. "And we're hoping that Tardon will understand an accidental intrusion."

"Hopefully," Gavin said. "By the time he figures things out, we'll be long gone."

Jack looked at Gavin. They were on the same page; maybe there was more to this guy than Jack thought.

"Okay," Benny said. "We'll speak to the Gnomes and see if they're willing."

"They look ready to fight to me," Gavin said.

"Oh, they are ready to fight," Benny said. "But asking them to act as bait is something much different."

Thirty

The group returned to the passage. Maddie was exhausted from self-projecting, and she found a spot to sit by herself. She leaned back and closed her eyes and was quickly joined by Lisa. Jack saw this and decided he would need to keep a closer watch on his newfound aunt. Benny quickly located Chief Eton, Retta, Fala, and Togo. He gathered them away from the others and was joined by Jack, Gavin, and Connie.

"Chief Eton," Benny began. "I have to ask yet another favor—one that will require you to put yourself and your people at great risk."

"Our homes, our friends, and our families have already been put at great risk by the one you call Tardon," Chief Eton said. "I'm sure what you have to ask will not be too much."

"Yeah," Gavin said. "I wouldn't be so sure about that, Chief."

Benny glared at Gavin. "We need to get into Tardon's village to rescue our friends, and we need a distraction."

"You'd like us to create some type of disturbance?" Chief Eton asked.

"That's what we were hoping," Benny said. "Would it be out of the ordinary for some of your Gnomes to happen upon this village, by accident of course?"

"My Gnomes," Chief Eton said. "Spend a lot of time gathering and exploring various mountains in this range. The mountains are vast and for some of us to discover something new and be curious about it wouldn't be that unexpected."

"But you'd have to allow Tardon to discover that you were there, and we would have very serious questions," Connie said.

"I understand."

"Your lives could be at risk," Jack said.

"I realize this," Chief Eton said. "But our lives are already at risk."

"So then, you're willing?" Benny asked.

"Of course," Chief Eton answered. "Whatever we can do to help restore the balance of things will be our pleasure."

"Thank you, Chief," Benny said. "Pick up some of your finest people and we'll plan this. We'd like to be ready to move by first daylight."

Chief Eton nodded and went back to his Gnomes to inform them of these new developments; Togo and Fala went with him.

"That was easy," Jack said.

"It was," Gavin agreed. "Let's hope planning and executing will be easy as well."

Lisa had sat with Maddie while the discussion with the Gnomes was taking place. She had closed her eyes, but was listening very closely. She had also heard Chief Eton tell the Gnomes of this plan and pick out six Gnomes to take part. She needed to take action, and as soon as everyone had fallen asleep, she made her way out of the passage.

Lisa paused at the opening to look back and make sure she hadn't disturbed anyone, and then she quietly moved outside. She found a spot away from the opening where, if anyone came out, she wouldn't be seen. She sat down and closed her eyes. Within a few seconds a nearly transparent image of Lisa stepped out of the real Lisa, leapt into the air, and flew down to Tardon's village. The image landed outside the largest building and then passed through the door without opening it.

The building looked like a meeting hall. It was one large room with a large wooden table at the center, and there were several people seated around it. All of them were dressed in red cloaks, and Tardon was seated at the head of the table. He smiled when he saw the image of Lisa enter.

"My friends," Tardon said. "We have a message."

The image stepped before Tardon and spoke. "I bring you a warning," it said. "The twins know where you are keeping their parents and are planning a rescue attempt. They will use the Gnomes to distract you and make a raid on the village."

Tardon laughed. "They are very foolish," he said. "But perhaps we should allow their plan to succeed. Yes, we will remove all protections and allow the twins to lead everyone in. Let them believe they have saved their parents, and then, when they are about to run to freedom, we will be waiting." He laughed again and everyone around the table joined in.

"As you wish," the image Lisa said, and then vanished.

The real Lisa opened her eyes. She looked around quickly to make certain she was alone, then stood and quietly returned to the passage. Once back inside, she returned to her place by Maddie, leaned back against the rock wall, and closed her eyes.

Thirty-One

Jack was up before the first morning light, and he left the safety of the passage. He climbed onto one of the large rocks just outside and sat there looking at the small village below. Though he shivered slightly, it wasn't the cold that he felt, but the uncertainty of things to come. For the first time, he'd begun to think about the consequences of this recue. What if his parents were killed? What if all the people who were helping him were killed? What if? Jack shook his head. He didn't even want to consider the possibility, but he had to face it. What if Maddie were killed?

"No," he said out loud. "That's one thing I will not let happen, no matter what.

He looked up and saw that the sun was beginning to come up over the mountains. The first rays of the morning light hit the tops of the mountains, and Jack suddenly realized how beautiful the world was. He heard a rustling behind him and turned quickly. Jack was relieved to see a familiar face.

"Good morning, Togo," he said.

Togo nodded. "Good morning, young sir," he said. "Please forgive me for a moment, I must thank the Great Mother before I begin my day."

Togo knelt and looked toward the sunrise, and then he bowed his head. His lips moved but Jack could not hear the words. Then, Togo bowed, kissed the ground, and stood. He climbed on top of the rock and sat beside Jack.

"So, you too are an early riser," Togo said.

"Not usually," Jack admitted. "I just have a lot to think about."

"Yes," Togo said. "I would imagine so. After all, your parents are being held against their will, your wizarding powers are new to you, and, excuse me for saying so, but is seems that your sister has latched onto someone of questionable background. It's quite a bit for someone so young to have to deal with."

"I take it that you're no fan of Lisa's?" Jack asked.

"I've heard stories that would make me wish to distance myself from her," Togo said. "However, Benny seems to have welcomed her, and I trust him."

"I'm not so sure that Benny's welcomed her," Jack said. "I think she's kind of forced herself on us."

Togo gave a small laugh. "I could see that happening."

Jack smiled as an idea that would allow him to focus more closely on the rescue mission came to him. "Can I ask you a favor?" he asked.

"There is no harm in asking," Togo said.

"I was wondering if you could keep an eye on Lisa, and maybe listen to the conversations she has with Maddie, and..."

"Not tell anyone I'm doing it," Togo finished.

Jack smiled again. "Exactly."

"If it will help to ease your mind, I will do my best."

"Thank you, Chief Togo," Jack said and stood on top of the rock. He looked down on the village again. "Come on," he said. Let's get this rescue under way."

Togo also stood. "Then you do have a plan?" he asked.

Other than having the Gnomes create a disturbance, Jack hadn't even considered a plan after that. So, he was surprised when he answered. "Yes, I do."

Jack and Togo made their way back through the opening and into the passage. Some of the Mountain Gnomes were beginning to gather their things in preparation for the day's events. Maddie saw Jack and ran to him.

"I was worried when you weren't here," she said. "Are you okay?"

"Fine," Jack said. "I just needed some time to think." Jack raised his hands and spoke loudly. "Everyone," he said. "Can I have your attention?"

Everyone stopped what they were doing and looked at Jack. Benny and Gavin were especially interested.

"As you all know, my parents are being held just below in Tardon's village. Today, we will get them back. Chief Eton has agreed to help us with the first part of our plan," Jack turned to Eton. "Thank you, sir."

Chief Eton bowed his head toward Jack, and Jack continued to address the group.

"While that part of the plan is taking place, my sister and I will enter the village, find our parents, and release them. If we are discovered I will need everyone's help. I am asking that all of the Gnomes find hiding places near the village. If things should go wrong, your help will be needed in the form of an attack. Can you do that?"

The Gnomes raised their hands and gave a shout of approval that brought a smile to Jack's face.

"Thank you," Jack said. "I ask my fellow wizards to enter the village with us and to act as cover. Watch our backs while we do what we have to. Again, thank you, all. Please be ready to go in five minutes."

Maddie grabbed Jack by the arm. "Why didn't you talk about this with me?" she said. "Why are you making all of these decisions without me?"

Jack looked over Maddie's shoulder at Lisa. "I would have, Sis," he said. "But you have this permanent shadow."

Maddie turned and saw that Lisa was very close by. She shook her head, but had no time to go back at her brother, as Benny, Gavin, and Connie already surrounded him.

"Are you out of your mind?" Benny asked. "Do you really think that you and Maddie are going to be able to just stroll into Tardon's village, get Ray and Tina, and just stroll back out?"

"Yes," he said. "I do."

"Jack," Connie said. "You're being foolish."

"Am I?" Jack asked. "Think about it. Maddie's image went into the village and nothing happened, and Tardon's gone through a lot of trouble to put his hideout where no one could find it. Why would it need a magical alarm system if no one knows where it is?"

"Jack," Benny warned. "It's time you left this to us."

"Well that's not going to happen," Jack assured Benny. "So just help me my way and we'll get this done."

Gavin took hold of Benny's arm. "A word please," he said, and led Benny off to the side by themselves. Gavin spoke softly. "I hate to admit," he said. "But the kid may be on to something. Tardon's just arrogant enough to think no one could find this village, and I think he wants the twins to find him anyway. Having the rest of the Gnomes nearby is a good idea; let his plan play out, and we'll just be ready to take over when the need arises."

Benny looked down and let out a long breath. He looked at Gavin. "Okay," he said. "Just be ready for anything. If Tardon wants them to come, he may have something planned for when they do."

"I'm sure he will," Gavin said. "He just doesn't know when we're coming."

Thirty-Two

The six Gnomes that Chief Eton chose for the distraction moved out before everyone else; the rest of the Gnomes left shortly after to take up their positions in the mountains surrounding Tardon's village. Jack made sure that everyone else was ready.

"Everyone knows the plan," he said. "When Maddie and I get into the village, be ready for anything."

Gavin shook his head, not unnoticed by Benny.

"Is something wrong?" Benny asked him.

"No," Gavin said. "I love suicide plans."

"Don't worry," Benny said. "I'm making arrangements to tilt things in our favor."

Gavin smiled at Benny and moved out of the passage. Benny held Connie back.

"I need you to get a message to Stanton," Benny said. "Let him know what we're about to do, and tell him to act accordingly."

Connie nodded and once outside, she went behind a group of rocks.

Once everyone else was outside, Jack came over to Benny. "The Gnomes are going to give us time to get down to the village before they act, then we'll go in."

Benny let out a slow breath. "I hope this works; you're putting a lot of people at risk."

"Don't think for a second that I haven't thought of that," Jack said. "Everyone here knows what can happen and I have thanked them. If I'm right, this will all be over very quickly." *And I'll be home before it gets dark,* he finished in his head.

Jack moved to where Maddie was standing with Lisa. "Listen, Maddie," Jack said. "If things don't go well, I want you to get out of there as fast as you can."

"Stop it, Jack," Maddie said. "I'm in this to the end, no matter what."

"I just want you to be safe," Jack said.

"I told you before," Maddie said. "I can take care of myself, and I don't need you bossing me around. You're not my father, Jack."

She began to walk away, but Jack grabbed her arm. "You listen to me," he said sternly. "If Dad were here, he'd tell you the same thing. Now do what I say, and if trouble breaks out, you get out of there."

"Let go of me," Maddie said as she pulled her arm from Jack's grasp. "I don't like who you've become, Jack. I don't know what you're trying to prove, but you're not the Jack I know."

"You're right," Jack said without hesitation. "I'm different, and it's out of necessity. You, of all people, should understand that." He looked at Lisa. "But maybe you're listening to someone else now."

Lisa looked at the ground; she wanted to avoid a confrontation.

"Don't you start, Jack," Maddie said. "Aunt Lisa's the only one who's shown any level of caring to me at all...."

"She's *Aunt Lisa* now?" Jack interrupted. "You better be careful who you put your trust in, and remember who really cares about you."

"I know who cares about me," Maddie snapped, and she took a slow, deep breath. "Are we going to do this or what?"

Jack looked at Lisa again and then at Maddie. "Just remember what I said." He turned to the group. "Are we ready?"

Everyone nodded, and they began walking to the village below. Jack stopped Lisa. "You can stay here; I don't think you'll be needed," he said.

Lisa thrust her nose in the air. "Listen to me, young man," she said. "If you think, for one second, that I'm going to sit back and do nothing while my family attempts something that may cost them their lives, you are very mistaken. Because my brother's not here to do it himself, I will make sure you two are safe, whether you like it or not."

Jack looked at the group moving away from him and he had no time to argue. "Fine," he said. "But stay in the back, and don't go into the village."

Lisa didn't answer and Jack hurried to the head of the group.

Lisa moved beside Maddie. "That's one very strong-willed boy," she said.

Maddie smiled. "Tell me about it," she said. "He makes me so angry sometimes. We're the same age, and he treats me like I'm his baby sister."

Lisa put an arm around Maddie. "You know," she said. "There comes a time when we all need to do what's best for ourselves. Maybe now is your time."

Maddie stopped and looked at Lisa and then at the group ahead of them. "Maybe," she said. "Let's catch up."

It was still very early when they reached the village and the morning mist hung in the air like an ominous fog. The wizards moved as quietly as they could to the back wall, just as the Gnomes approached the front gate. After a few seconds, Jack heard the Gnomes talking loudly among themselves. He couldn't make out every word, but it sounded like they were discussing the discovery of a village in their mountains, and they weren't happy about it.

Jack peeked over the wall. The Gnomes had gotten the attention of the dragons that had taken to the air and were circling over the gate as if awaiting an order to attack. The Gnomes began to talk even louder. They pointed at the dragons and Jack knew there was true fear in their voices. Suddenly, the door to the largest building burst open, and a dozen people cloaked in red ran toward the front gate.

"Maddie!" Jack called. "Let's move."

Maddie came to Jack's side, as did Connie.

"Connie," Jack said. "Stay here with the others."

"I don't think so, Jack," Connie said. "I'm coming with you."

"So am I," Gavin said.

"Me too," Benny chimed in.

Jack threw his hands in the air. "Way to stick to a plan," he mumbled. He looked at the commotion at the front gate. "Fine; let's move. Everyone keep an eye out while me and Maddie get to the small building."

No one said a word as they climbed over the wall and headed toward the building where Ray and Tina were being held.

Maddie, Jack, and Connie made their way to the front door while the others did their best to stay out of sight. The yelling at the front gate had become even louder. The wizards in red were demanding to know what the Gnomes were doing there, and the Gnomes wanted to know why they'd built a village without permission.

Jack pulled on the front door of the small building but it didn't open. Connie put a hand on the door and it gave way. They hurried inside and saw Ray and Tina sitting on a dirt floor in the far corner of the room. Tina looked up and her eyes went wide. She leapt to her feet and ran to the twins, hugging both of them at the same time.

"I'm so happy to see you two," she said. "How did you get in here?"

Jack pulled away from his mother's welcoming embrace. "There's no time to explain now," he said. "We have to get out of here."

Ray had also gotten up from the floor and was now standing beside his family. "Jack's right," he said. "We can get caught up later."

They ran to the door and were met by Benny and Gavin; Lisa was a few steps behind them.

"I'm glad to see there's backup," Tina said. "I was afraid these two had taken this upon themselves."

"They kind of have," Benny said. "But we can fill you in later."

Ray saw Lisa at the rear of the group and he took hold of Benny's shoulder. "What is *she* doing here?" he asked.

"Helping," Gavin said. "Now, can we please move?"

Ray accepted his sister's presence for that moment, and hurried with the others toward the back wall of the village. The yelling at the gate had escalated, and more of the Tars were coming out of the large building.

Benny stopped. "We're going to have to help them," he said.

"We will," Jack said. "Let's get Maddie and my parents over the wall, and then we'll go back."

Lisa was first over the wall and she held out a hand to Tina. Tina hesitated, and when she finally reached out her hand to get over the wall, she felt something hit her and fell back, hitting the ground hard.

Ray and Jack turned and saw that they were facing twenty red-cloaked figures, and in the center, his white hair blowing around his face, was Tardon.

"It seems my guests were leaving without saying goodbye," Tardon said. "I find that quite rude."

Benny reached out his hand, but before anything could be done, a swipe of Tardon's arm froze all of them in their spots.

"There will be none of that," Tardon said.

Thirty-Three

Tardon turned to his followers. "Bound the Gnomes and bring them to the hall," he said, and pointed to Maddie. "Take the girl." Then he pointed to Lisa. "And that one to the cell. Bring the rest into the hall," he said and walked away.

A dozen of Tardon's followers encircled Maddie and Lisa. A very large one pushed Lisa and another grabbed Maddie.

"Don't you touch her!" Jack yelled, and another one of the Tars pushed him hard to the ground.

Jack looked up and he felt the temperature of his blood tick up a few degrees. He wanted so badly to do something, anything, but he knew it would be useless at this point. Connie rushed to his side and helped him back to his feet.

"Keep your cool here, Jack," Connie said. "Our lives depend on it."

Jack clenched his teeth. He knew she was right; he just hoped that the Gnomes hiding in the mountains would realize that not all had gone as planned.

"Let's move!" one of the Tars yelled. "Tardon wants you in the hall, and you don't want to keep him waiting." The other Tars laughed as the group was forced to walk into the large building.

Ray moved close to Benny. "I hope this isn't all you had planned," he whispered.

"No," Benny said. "This is all Jack had planned. He is the mastermind here."

"That's just great," Ray said. "Then I guess we'll have to make this up as we go."

The large hall was just that: a very large room with a long wooden table in the center of it. It reminded Jack of something out of a middle-ages-themed movie, where the warriors gathered for a feast after a great victory. The Tars made them sit on the floor against a side wall. Tardon sat in a large chair at the head of the table, and his followers filled the smaller chairs around the table—except for the Tars keeping a close watch on the prisoners.

In a few seconds, the six Mountain Gnomes were brought in. Their hands were tied behind their backs and their mouths were covered with cloth. They were made to sit on the floor on the other side of the room from the wizards.

Tardon looked around the room. "Well," he said in a sinister whisper. "Here we have six intruders." He inclined his head toward the Gnomes. "And some would-be rescuers," he pointed at the wizards. "What shall we do with them?"

Jack got up. "Where is my sister?" he demanded, and was immediately pushed to the ground again.

Tina moved to Jack. "Don't you touch my son," she said, shielding him.

One of the Tars reached out to grab Tina, and Ray rose quickly to push him aside. The Tars rose from the table as one and several of the nearby guards surrounded Ray.

"Easy," Tardon said. "Let's not have any one lose control here; it will only make things worse for all of you. After all, even the *destined ones* can't take on all of us."

The Tars laughed and Jack looked around, confused.

Tardon stood and walked in front of his prisoners. "You really should relax, Tina dear," he said. "Your son will be fine." He looked to his followers. "For now." The room erupted in laughter as Tardon returned to his seat. "As for your inquiry, young man, your sister is in no danger at the moment and she has company. I believe it would be best if you just worried about yourself for now."

Jack felt his body temperature go up another degree. He looked at Connie as she mouthed the words "Stay cool" to him.

While Jack was being warned to keep his emotions under control, Maddie was losing control of her own. She and Lisa had been placed in the small building she had freed her parents from. There was a small window, and Maddie stared out of it, wondering what was happening to the others. Tears ran down her cheeks.

"We have to get out of here," she said.

Lisa shook her head. "Look around. I don't think we can go anywhere."

Lisa was right. Just outside were three Tars and many more patrolled the grounds of the village.

"But we have to help them," Maddie argued through her tears. "There has to be a way."

Lisa sighed. "All we can do now is keep an eye out to see if an opening arises, but I have to be honest: I don't see how we can help them."

Maddie looked out of the window again and then turned back to Lisa. "Maybe I can project myself and find out what's going on."

"Don't you think they'd see that?" Lisa questioned. "You would only put us in greater danger." She walked over to Maddie and put an arm around her. "You have to accept that there's nothing we can do right now."

Maddie did her best Jack imitation and yelled. "How can I accept that? My whole family is that building and I need to know what's going on!"

"You can't put yourself and the rest of us at risk," Lisa said. "It's best if we just stay here and wait."

Maddie took a deep breath and sat down on the floor. She buried her head in her folded arms and cried.

Tardon paced slowly around the large table in the hall. "We must set an example," he said. "Intrusions must not be tolerated." He stopped in front of the Gnomes. "Trespassers must be dealt with, and since these Gnomes have made it clear that they have taken sides against us, we must send a message to all of them." He stroked his long beard. "Perhaps a good old-fashioned hanging will send the proper message." He pointed to two of the Tars. "Ready the courtyard for an execution."

The two Tars left the hall and the others laughed.

Jack's legs began to shake, and he looked at his parents. "Do something," he whispered.

"What can we do?" Ray asked in a barely audible voice. "We're heavily outnumbered. Any move would get us all killed."

Jack swallowed hard, and looked at Benny. "Do you have any ideas?"

Benny looked at Jack and had a surprisingly calm expression. "Yes," he said. "Patience."

Jack decided to take matters into his own hands. "You can't do that!" he yelled.

Tardon looked at Jack and walked slowly, stopping right in front of him. Tardon held Jack's chin and bent so he could look into his eyes. "Listen to me, young *destined one*," Tardon said. "I can, and I will, and you can do nothing to stop me. It seems that this talk of the ones of destiny was just that: mere talk." This brought more laughter from the Tars.

Jack pulled away from Tardon's grip. "Don't you touch me, you coward," he said.

"Coward?" Tardon asked.

"Yes, coward," Jack answered. "You have all of these people here to help you, and you choose to pick on those who can't defend themselves. I'd like to see what you'd

218

do one-on-one, but looking around, I don't think you have the guts."

Tardon smiled. "Are you challenging me? Perhaps it is true then; perhaps you are one of the *destined ones*."

"Why do you keep saying that?" Jack asked.

Tardon looked into Jack's eyes. "You truly don't know, do you?" Tardon looked at Benny. "Benjamin," he said. "I'm quite surprised that you haven't told him."

"Told me what?" Jack demanded.

"Nothing," Tina said. "He's just trying to upset you."

Tardon laughed and looked at Tina. "Nothing, is it? Is it nothing that when your twins were born, it was said that they would be great and powerful, that they would unite the magical realm and save the world?" He looked at Jack. "Do *you* think that's nothing?"

Jack looked at his parents. "Is it true?"

They both looked at the floor. Jack turned to Benny. "Is that what you've been hiding? Is that why you brought us here?"

"I brought you here so you could help save your parents," Benny said.

One of the Tars entered the room. "The courtyard is ready," he announced.

"Excellent," Tardon said. "Your discussion will have to wait." He turned to the room. "Bring everyone outside for the hanging."

The Tars forced everyone out into the courtyard. From the window in the small building, Maddie could see Jack being pushed along as a large crowed formed outside.

"Something's going on," she said.

Lisa looked out the window. She took note of the gallows and saw the Gnomes being forced toward them. She turned away from the window. "It looks like Tardon is going to hang the Gnomes," she said.

"No!" Maddie screamed. "What can we do?"

"Look at the size of the crowd," Lisa said. "There is nothing we can do."

Jack stood beside Benny and his father as the Gnomes had nooses placed around their necks. The Gnomes were standing on a ledge several feet off the ground, and Jack knew that once it was removed, they would be strangled to death.

Jack looked at his father. "It doesn't matter what happens to us; we have to do something," he said.

Ray looked at Benny. "You know that he's right," he said.

"Do you propose that we place ourselves in death's path?" Benny asked.

"They did it for us," Jack said. "I won't just stand here and watch them die."

Tardon addressed the crowd from beside the gallows. "Let this be a message for all who oppose us," he said. "We have ushered in a new era, and it will not be stopped."

Tardon raised his arm, and Jack knew that when it fell so would the Gnomes. He took a deep breath and raised his hand, but before he could act, the ropes around the Gnomes vanished and a loud, powerful voice called out from the front gate.

"Tardon, you will release the Gnomes, and my friends."

All eyes turned toward the gate. Standing there, the sun reflecting off his white cloak, was Stanton, and he had brought an army.

Cris Pasqueralle

Thirty-Four

Tardon and Stanton looked at each other. "I do not take orders from you," Tardon said. "And you are far from your territory."

"Anywhere magic is being abused is my territory," Stanton answered. "And you have been abusing magic for far too long." Stanton turned to the army behind him. "Take them," he commanded.

A wave of white rushed into the small village, followed by the forest and Mountain Gnomes, who were led by Togo, Fala, Chief Eton, and Retta. They were met by forces in red, streaming from the buildings that made up the village. It seemed impossible that the buildings could hold so many, but their numbers were equal to that of Stanton's.

Ray grabbed Jack as he was about to join the fray. "Get out of here, Jack," he said. "Go hide in the mountains, and I'll find you later."

Jack pulled away from his father. "No," he said. "I brought the Gnomes here to help save you. I have a responsibility to them, and I won't hide while they fight." He turned his back to Ray and headed for the gallows where the Gnomes, though free from the ropes around their necks, were still tied.

As Jack ran, a large hole opened in the ground in front of him. He pushed off the ground hard and took flight, landing on the gallows. He ran to each of the Gnomes and placed his hand on the ropes tying their hands, freeing them.

One of the Gnomes took Jack's hand. "We know who you are, and why you are here," he said. "We would have died for you."

Jack's jaw fell open. Why would anyone be willing to die for him? A part of the rock wall behind Jack exploded into tiny pebbles, pulling him from his thoughts. "Go!" he said to the Gnomes, and they joined their fellow Gnomes in the fight.

From the ledge on the gallows, Jack scanned the village. Wizards in white were fighting wizards in red, most with magic, some in hand-to-hand combat. He saw Gavin put up a hand and send one of the Tars flying right out of the village. Benny paralyzed a group of Tars with a wave of his hand, and his parents pushed aside combatants with ease. Jack pumped his fist at the sight of his parents' power. He looked around further and saw that Connie was more than holding her own, but Maddie was nowhere to be seen.

From the window of the cell, Maddie saw a large number of people in white charge into the village. "Something's happening out there," she said, and Lisa hurried to the window.

Lisa saw the battle begin as wizards in red clashed with those in white. The ground shook as magic met magic head on. Lisa turned from the window. "It appears Stanton has come to save us," she said, without emotion.

"That's great," Maddie said. "This is our chance to get out of here." She made a move toward the door, but Lisa stopped her.

"No," Lisa said. "I can't let you go out there. I'd never forgive myself if something happened to you. We'll wait for them to come to us."

There were loud voices just outside the window, and Maddie took another look. Gavin had been taken to the ground by one of the Tars and was bleeding from the head.

"Come on!" Gavin yelled. "Just try and finish me!"

The large man laughed. "I will finish you," he said, and raised both hands. Gavin leapt to his feet and waved his arm. The man froze for a second and then his body appeared to fold into smaller and smaller sections until it just disappeared. Gavin let out a roar and screamed to all who could hear. "Who's next?"

Maddie stepped back from the window with her eyes wide, holding her hand over her mouth. Lisa looked at her and went to the window.

Stanton strode confidently through the battle, sweeping his arms as he walked and toppling Tars left and right. Lisa looked past Stanton and saw her brother in a fistfight with a large Tar and Tina, calling forth a whirlwind of dust to obstruct the vision of two Tars in pursuit of her. Lisa stepped away from the window.

Jack saw Connie and he leapt from the ledge of the gallows and ran toward her.

It's one of the *destined ones!*" a voice yelled, and the Tars within earshot turned their attention to Jack.

Clumps of dirt flew everywhere as they sent spells in his direction. Jack slid as if he were stealing second base, turned toward the source of the magic, popped to his feet, and thrust a fist toward the opposition.

As if hit by a cannon blast, four of the Tars fell back and hit the ground hard. Jack felt a hand on his shoulder and turned, ready to defend himself. He heaved in relief when he saw it was Connie.

"Nice shot, Jack," she said, and he managed to give her a smile.

"Who are all of these people?" Jack asked.

"Stanton's guard," Connie answered. "And, Stanton."

"How did he know we were here?"

"Benny doesn't leave things to chance," Connie said. "He had me send a message before we left this morning."

Jack looked at the ground.

"Are you mad?" Connie asked.

Jack looked at her. "No, not with the way things turned out," he said. "Have you seen Maddie?"

"No," Connie said. "We don't know where they're keeping her."

"I have to find her," Jack said. "And I would guess they have her where they had Mom and Dad." He ran toward the small building.

"Wait!" Connie yelled. "I'm coming with you."

Tardon had made his way to the roof of the large building and was raining damage on all below him. He took out a small group of Stanton's guard, and when several Gnomes attempted to rush toward him, Tardon sent a fireball into their midst. The ensuing explosion sent several Gnomes into the air, and when the debris settled, the bodies of the Gnomes were scattered about, including the body of Chief Eton. The blast had sent Jack and Connie ducking for cover, and when they raised their heads, they saw the carnage before them.

Connie caught sight of Chief Eton's lifeless body. "No!" Connie yelled and she ran toward the body, with Jack right behind her.

They got to it just as Retta did. Retta knelt at her father's side and a tear made a path down her cheek.

Connie put a hand on her shoulder. "I'm so sorry," she said.

Retta stood. "He belongs to our Great Mother now," she said. "There is nothing we can do for him except to make sure he died for something." And just like that, she rejoined the fight.

Jack and Connie looked at each other and shrugged at the same time.

Tardon caught sight of Jack below him. "So, destined one," he called. "Have for you come for me now?"

Jack looked up at Tardon. With his long white hair blowing around his face, and his cloak billowing behind him, Tardon appeared to be a madman, laughing while people died around him. Jack took a deep breath.

Connie grabbed his arm. "Jack, you're not ready."

Jack shrugged. "It has to happen some time," he said, and moved toward the building.

Tardon saw Jack walk toward him and he let out a laugh that just reinforced Jack's notion of him being a madman. "Then you *have* come for me," Tardon said.

A voice called back to Tardon from behind Jack. "No, he hasn't, but I have."

It was Tina, and she gave no time for discussion as she immediately began sending waves of spells at Tardon. He laughed and moved across the rooftop, repelling all of Tina's efforts.

"Are you going to force me to kill you in front of your children?" Tardon challenged. "Think of what kind of memory that would be for them. Give yourself up, and I will kill you quickly, away from everyone so that no one will see you beg for mercy."

"I would never beg you for anything!" Tina yelled back, as she sent a whirlwind at Tardon that knocked him slightly off balance. She quickly took advantage and sent another spell that brought Tardon down to one knee.

From the cell room, Maddie felt an explosion and saw the light of the blast come through the window. She looked out and saw the bodies of the Gnomes lying about like storm-blown yard debris.

"We need to help," Maddie said and she ran out the door. Lisa went after her.

"Maddie, stop!" Lisa yelled, and since Maddie didn't know where to go or what to do, she stopped. Lisa moved close and put both hands on Maddie's shoulders. "You can't get involved in this; you have to stay out of danger."

Maddie pulled away from Lisa. "My family is in danger; I need to help them, now."

"No, Maddie. Not here, not now."

"Everyone has to stop trying to protect me," Maddie said. "I can take care of myself."

"I know that," Lisa said. "But you have a great destiny, and it must be seen to fulfillment. For the good of magic, and the world."

Maddie shook her head several times, and she looked at Lisa with her eyes squinted. "What are you talking about?" she asked.

Lisa took a deep breath. "The necklace you wear: look at it."

Maddie pulled the necklace from beneath her shirt. "It's a globe. So what?"

"It's the Earth," Lisa said. "And I believe Jack was given the Sun."

"So?"

"So," Lisa said. "The Sun is a star and stars burn out, but the Earth is a rock and rocks are solid. We build our foundations on solid rock. You are the Earth, the solid rock that magic will build its foundation on. You are the one destined to rule over all the realms, the one destined to lead magic, and control all the realms."

Maddie was overwhelmed.

"But Uncle Benny said the realms couldn't mix; that magic in the non-magic would destroy the world."

"That's not right," Lisa said. "It is the *destined one* who can unite the realms and bring magic to its rightful place. You are that *one*."

Maddie didn't say anything; she simply stood there staring at nothing. She heard a scream of pain and turned to see another Gnome fall at the hands of one of the Tars.

Lisa grabbed Maddie's hand. "Come on; I need to get you out of here," she said, and she closed her eyes, and they both vanished.

Tardon regained his balance and jumped from the roof, floating gently to the ground. He waved his hand, and a shield placed in front of her by Ray deflected a spell that would have hit Tina.

"None of my family dies by your hand today, Tardon," Ray said.

Tardon laughed. "Your whole family may die by my hand before the day is over," he said.

"I don't think so," Gavin said, as he lined up next to Ray and Tina.

"Neither do I," Benny said, as he joined the group.

"How nice," Tardon mocked. "Now everyone has joined the party." He clapped his hands and dozens of his followers lined up behind him. "You see," he said. "You cannot match my forces."

"I believe we can," Stanton said as he stepped forward with a large number of his white cloaked guard.

"Now the party can truly begin," Tardon said. "But I must take care of a previous matter first." He waved his hand, and Tina was sent flying into the gallows.

She bounced off the top beam, and the whole contraption came down on top of her as she hit the ground. At the same time, the Tars attacked, matched by Stanton's guard. Connie joined the attack, and she, Gavin, Benny, and Ray each took on several Tars, while Stanton went after Tardon, who had fled into the large building. Jack saw that Tina had hit the gallows, and he went to her.

He dug through the splintered remains of the gallows to get to Tina. She had several cuts and bruises on her face and a large head wound that poured blood. Her eyes were closed.

"Mom, Mom," Jack said. "Talk to me, please." He gently tapped her cheek as tears ran down his own. "Come on, Mom, wake up," he pleaded while the battle raged around him.

The Tars were being driven from their village by the force of Stanton's guard. There was a loud *BANG!* and the doors of the large building flew into the courtyard, followed by two tornadoes. They swirled into the center of the courtyard and when they stopped, Stanton and Tardon were standing face to face.

Jack looked at his mother and then at the two men in the courtyard, and he felt the blood in his veins jump way past the boiling point. He kissed Tina on the forehead, and ran to the courtyard.

Stanton and Tardon stared at each other.

"You know that your end is near," Tardon said.

"I know no such thing," Stanton said. "I only know that no matter what happens here between you and I, you cannot win in the long-run."

233

Tardon laughed. "You truly believe in destiny, don't you," he said. "There is no such thing; we make our own destinies, and there is no way I will be defeated by two youngsters."

Jack ran between Stanton and Tardon and he looked directly into Tardon's eyes. "Why don't we find out right now," he challenged.

Tardon shook his head. "Don't be foolish, little boy," he said.

"Still acting the coward?" Jack questioned.

"Jack!" Ray yelled. "Now is not your time; let Stanton handle this."

"Now is the perfect time," Jack said, still staring at Tardon. "I challenged you before and it still stands, unless you are a coward."

Tardon took a step back. "If that's the way you want it, so be it."

"Jack," Stanton said. "Please."

"Back off," Jack warned. "He's mine."

Tardon raised a hand and a blast of cold air staggered Jack. Jack pointed at Tardon, but a swipe of his hand turned the spell away. Jack tried again, but Tardon blocked that attempt as well.

"You are nothing, little boy," Tardon said. "Why would you challenge me?"

Jack tried again but it was still nothing for Tardon to turn away his spell. Tardon raised a hand and Jack doubled over as though he were hit with a hard punch to the stomach. Another swipe of Tardon's hand, and Jack went down. Tardon walked toward Jack with both hands extended in front of him, and Jack writhed on the ground in obvious pain.

Tardon looked down at his victim. "You challenged me, and now you will die. Your sister will be next."

Jack's head throbbed with pain, and his blood raced through his body. "No!" he screamed, as he extended his hands and sent Tardon three feet into the air.

Tardon landed hard as Jack scrambled to his feet.

"You will never touch my sister!" Jack yelled, and he threw punches into the air like a boxer throwing lethal combinations.

Each thrust of Jack's hands drove Tardon back; they came so fast that Tardon could not retaliate. Finally, it was Tardon who was on the ground and in great pain. Jack continued the barrage, and a golden light came from his hands and entered Tardon's body like lightning bolts.

The Tars still in the village saw their leader on the ground, and each one made himself vanish. Tardon took a deep breath, and before Jack could land a fatal blow, he too vanished.

When Tardon disappeared, Jack let out a scream, and then he fell to the ground, unconscious.

Thirty-Five

Jack opened his eyes and found that he was back in the room he and Maddie had shared at Benny's house. This time, the bed across from his was occupied by Tina. Jack got out of bed and went over to his mother. He knelt beside her and looked at her closely. Tina's eyes were closed, and she breathed heavily. The wound on her head was gone, and she looked all right. Jack sighed and kissed her forehead.

"I'm glad you're okay, Mom," he whispered. "I love you very much."

He stood, looked at Tina for a few more seconds, and then left the room.

Jack stepped into the hall. His legs felt weak, and everything seemed to spin just a bit. He put his hand on the wall to steady himself and took in several long breaths. The spinning subsided and he heard voices coming from the kitchen. He stopped at the entrance to the kitchen to survey the scene. Ray, Benny, and Stanton were seated at the table, and Jack listened for a moment.

"We're going to have to let him know everything," Benny said.

Stanton nodded. "I agree.

"What about Maddie?" Ray asked. "We need to find her."

"We will," Stanton said. "The twins need to be united if the magical realm is going to be saved."

Ray stood. "I could care less about them saving the magical realm," he said. "The safety of my children is all that concerns me now."

"I'm glad to hear that," Jack said, as he walked slowly into the room.

Ray turned. "Jack, how are you feeling?" he asked as he pulled out a chair for his son, and they both sat.

"I'm a little sore," Jack replied. "But I'll be fine. How's Mom?"

"Tina will be just fine," Stanton said. "She needs plenty of rest."

"Good," Jack said. "So, where's Maddie?"

Ray exchanged glances with Benny and Stanton.

"I said, where's Maddie?" Jack asked again, more than a bit impatient.

Ray cleared his throat. "We, umm, don't know."

Jack bit his lower lip. "What do you mean, you don't know?"

"She disappeared with Lisa," Benny said. "Gavin and Connie are looking for them right now."

Jack ran his hands through his hair, trying to keep calm. "She's with Lisa," he said. "That's just great." He turned to his father. "Why are you sitting here? You should be out looking for her."

"I've been taking care of you and your mother," Ray said. "And don't you question me, young man."

Jack looked down for a second and snickered, and then he looked Ray directly in the eye. "Don't play Daddy with me right now," he said. "I don't need to be taken care of by you or anyone else. Now, let's stop all the lies and give me some straight answers."

Ray stood again, but so did Stanton. He put a hand on Ray's shoulder and eased him back to his seat. Stanton also returned to his seat.

"Jack is right," Stanton said. "He does deserve some answers," he gestured toward Jack with his hand. "Would you like to ask some questions?"

Jack didn't like the way he was being spoken to and his blood began to get warm. He swallowed hard and tried to keep his cool. "Sure," he said. "Tell me about this destiny thing. Why did Tardon keep calling me and Maddie the *destined ones*?"

"Because you are," Stanton said.

Jack looked at Stanton. This guy was really getting on his nerves. "I'm going to need a little more than that," he said.

"Of course," Stanton said. "Many years ago, a very powerful wizard began to speak of the importance of magic and how the magical realm should rule the world. He spoke about how it would be in the best interests of all the realms. Never once did he take into account the importance of the delicate balance nature has established between the realms. He never thought about how much instability and destruction could be caused by upsetting that balance."

"Let me guess," Jack said. "You're talking about Tardon."

"Yes," Stanton answered. "Over time, Tardon gained many followers and he was able to divide the magical realm and take control over half of it. Fortunately, I was able to persuade many that Tardon's ideas were dangerous, and together we were able to hold onto half the magical realm. But, Tardon is very powerful and it seemed that there would be no way to hold him in check for long. However, his focus became distracted. He learned of an ancient saying: that one with the power of two was destined to restore balance and order to all the realms. When you and your sister were born, he, along with many others, took it as a sign that together you and Maddie had the power of two."

"Because we're twins?" Jack asked.

"Exactly," Stanton confirmed. "Twins are a very rare thing in the magical realm. In fact, you may be the only ones. Great hope arose around your birth, from both Tardon and those who believed that you would be able to defeat him. It became too much, and I asked Ray and Tina to take you to the non-magical realm, to raise you away from all the attention, and away from Tardon. But, when your powers became evident, Tardon was able to feel your magic and discover where you were. When he came for you, he set in motion that events that have led us to this point."

"And why didn't anyone tell us this before?" Jack questioned.

"We planned to," Ray said. "Your mother and I wanted to be the ones to tell you. We hoped to ease you into it, and train you properly, but…"

"Tardon kidnapped you and you needed to be saved," Jack finished for his father.

Ray nodded.

"Okay," Jack said. "So let's forget about all of that for now, and let's concentrate on Maddie. Where do you think she is?"

Benny and Stanton looked at each other. Ray actually smiled at the concern Jack showed for his sister.

"We're not sure," Benny said. "We think that Tardon believes that keeping the two of you separated will keep your destiny from being fulfilled."

Jack shook his head. "Here we go again," he said. "So you think Tardon has Maddie?"

"In a sense," Stanton said. "We believe that Lisa has taken Maddie on Tardon's orders."

Jack's blood became too hot to handle, and he erupted. He kicked over the chair as he leapt to his feet. "So, Lisa *is* one of his followers!" Jack yelled, and turned to Benny. "And you let her close to my sister!" He lunged across the table in an effort to get at Benny, but Ray held him back.

"Take it easy, Son," Ray said.

Jack turned on his father. "Son?" he asked. "You've been a part of this all along; you raised us to save your magical realm. Don't call me *son*."

Ray let go of Jack and fell into his chair. He hung his head.

Jack turned his anger on all of them. "I hate to disappoint all of you," he said. "But I will not be a part of any destiny. I don't even want to be a part of your magical world or have anything to do with any of you. You're all a bunch of liars, interested in yourselves." He looked at Ray. "And you were willing to put me and Maddie in danger to protect something we didn't even know existed..." Jack didn't finish; he couldn't. He took a deep breath and headed for the door.

"Jack!" Benny called. "Where are you going?"

"Away from all of this," Jack said. "I don't want anything to do with it. You wizards are on your own." He walked out the door.

Ray, Benny, and Stanton went after him.

They stood in the moonlit forest, the damp cold latching onto them.

"Jack," Ray said. "You can't just leave."

"No?" Jack challenged. "Why not?"

"Because the magical realm is your true home," Stanton said. "And it needs you to survive."

"Sure it does," Jack said.

Benny stepped in front of Jack. "It's true," he said. "Our realm and all the others are in danger without you and Maddie. We need the two of you to survive."

Jack stepped within an inch of Benny. "You've done nothing but lie to me since you brought me to this place. I have no reason to believe you, and, just so you know, I'm holding you personally responsible for my sister's safety." Jack lowered his voice so only Benny could hear his next sentence. "You know what I'm capable of," he said. "You've seen what I can do. You find Maddie, and you bring her to me safely, or I'll find you."

Jack stepped away from Benny and walked into the dense forest.

"Jack!" Ray called. "Where are you going?"

Jack turned to face the three men. "To the world I know," he said, and he closed his eyes and was gone.

END ?

Dedication

For my wife Tricia, and my daughters Toniann and
Deanna.

You inspire me daily in so many ways.

About The Author

Cris Pasqueralle is a retired New York City police officer who has always had a passion and love for books. Writing one has been a life-long dream. It was his daughter's love of fantasy fiction that finally led Cris to pen The Destiny Trilogy. Cris enjoys writing Middle Grade and Young Adult because he believes that reading opens up a world of possibilities for young minds. Cris lives on Long Island New York with his wife and two daughters.

Follow Cris@

www.authorcrispasqueralle.weebly.com

Twitter:

@cpasqueralle

Facebook:

www.facebook.com/authorcrispasqueralle

Cosby Media Productions ™

Entertaining the Mind, and Inspiring the Soul

www.cosbymediaproductions.com